DEMON'D

David Berardelli

DEMON'D

GRAVESTONE PRESS

Gravestone Press
is an imprint of
Fiction4All
www.fiction4all.com

This Edition
Published 2022

CHAPTER 1 - THE DAY BEFORE

I never thought my destiny would change after a simple evening phone call from the folks.

All your life you hear things like, "If I had just done things a little differently…" Or "If I had been two minutes earlier…or later…" Or "If only my car hadn't started when it did…"

You hear all sorts of bullshit like that, usually when something unexpected happens, or when things go terribly wrong. Most of it deals with guilt or wish fulfillment. Someone didn't get his promotion because he pissed off the wrong guy. Or a woman was involved in a traffic accident because she stopped to buy a cruller when she should have been somewhere else. Or the guy who was just one number off with his LOTTO ticket because he cut in line and bought the wrong ticket.

But even so, you don't take any of it seriously.

At least, you try *not* to…

You put emphasis into such talk only if something horrible happens to you personally and you want to convince yourself that one simple and innocent factor might have prevented it.

In my own case, the phrase, "If I hadn't answered the phone," had been, in my humble opinion, the single factor that changed the entire course of my destiny. To make the situation even worse, the bizarre event took place at the kitchen table of my condo, while I was enjoying a succulent meal of chicken cordon blue and green bean casserole after putting in a hard day at the office.

My phone rang, and my first instinct was to enjoy my meal, *then* see who it was, and answer it—or *not* answer it. Half of me wanted to let it ring while the other half—that curious part that almost always get you in trouble—told me it might be important.

I checked the display and decided to answer it. It was from my folks, so I figured it would be all right, since I could engage in our usual small talk while enjoying my meal at the same time.

"I take it you heard about your high school friend dying," Mom said the moment she heard my voice.

I placed the cell on the table near my left elbow and had a sip of port wine.

"Which one?" I asked. This didn't by any means suggest that I had so many friends to consider. I had never been an athlete in high school. Consequently, I hadn't been a member of the "Circle"—that esteemed group of arrogant, narcissistic, self-appointed individuals associated with sports and scholastic achievement—a clique exuding colossal popularity and an almost godlike façade amongst the commoners. To make my social position even worse, I had been a musician, playing trumpet for four years in the high school band.

The topic of this conversation, to me, could not have been more irrelevant. I graduated more than twenty years earlier, fashioned a respectable career in software, and had severed all ties from my high school years. Any friendships I had made during this time had long since died from gross neglect and simple indifference.

In short, my memory needed slightly more coaxing.

"Who are we talking about?" I asked.

"What was his name, Andrew?" my mom asked. "Caliban? Cavendish?"

I could well imagine my dad's irritation as he nibbled on whatever they were having for dinner. Knowing them as I did, it was either a medium rare T-bone and baked potato, or a juicy pork chop and seasoned curly fries.

Since they were on speaker, I heard him say "Cavanaugh. Bruce Cavanaugh, I believe." Then he went silent. I could easily imagine him nibbling on his entrée, then having a slug of Michelob, his favorite beverage. His belch made me smile behind my wine glass.

Bruce Cavanaugh. The name instantly twanged a cloud of unpleasant familiarity. Cavanaugh had always been considered our class zero, the sort of non-entity most people ignore or make fun of. He was the boy everyone snubbed in class and on the street. Always daydreaming and never one to pay attention, he was held back for two years because of poor attendance and abysmal grades. Propped up immeasurably by his prowess on the track, he eventually graduated.

Since he had spent most of his childhood dodging bullies, he developed quick instincts and had regularly done the hundred-yard dash in less than ten seconds. In twelfth grade, Cavanaugh, at twenty, was five-eight, weighed in at around one-twenty, and could outrun anyone. For some strange reason, he singled me out as his best and only friend from the third grade on and stuck to me like Velcro until graduation day, when, thank God, we finally went our separate ways.

"How about that? Cavanaugh's, well, dead..." It was difficult, keeping the word "finally" out of the sentence. I found it awkward to contain my sense of relief. Although I tried keeping the smile from taking over, my impulsive reaction had won out, clearly revealing my emotions.

My mother said, "You don't sound very sad, Frank..."

"Yeah." My father had also picked up on my obvious lack of remorse. "Sounds like ya just won the Lottery."

I had nothing to say, so I didn't say anything.

"Wasn't he that little jerk," my father asked a moment later, "used to ride over here on his bike from the other side of town to see ya when you two were in grade school?"

I tried to hold back the groan but was unsuccessful.

"Frank? Your father just asked you a question."

"That was him, all right."

"Didn't ya used to hide in your room when we told ya he was here?"

"Yeah..."

"We always figured you didn't like him much," Mom said.

"He seemed weird," Dad added.

"He was," I said. "He always got me in trouble."

"Is he the boy, carved your initials on your third-grade teacher's desk?" Mom asked. "Then she called and asked one of us to come to the school and have a talk with your principal?"

"That was him." Even after thirty years, I found myself getting angry all over again.

If only Cavanaugh had left me alone in those days...

If only he'd stopped bugging me...

But he didn't. He stuck to me like a tick on a dog and, once he'd completed his second run-through of sixth grade and made it to junior high, stayed right there, at my side.

After that, things got worse.

In grade school, bonding is a simple process. The "misery loves company" mentality becomes the norm. A kid needs a feeling of belonging among another kids. It could be as simple as both kids being the same size or having the same hair color. Or even the minor matter of living on the same street. In many cases, two boys becoming prime targets for the playground bully could be all it takes to form a kinship.

In high school, however, the process transforms into something slightly more complicated. There are more kids involved, and their frontal lobes have developed a little in the last year or so. Attitudes are more prevalent. Temperaments have progressed, most of them negatively.

The submissive, in this case, has become much more isolated. His standing and reputation have suffered, and he is forced to struggle to maintain whatever friendship he has managed to develop.

Cavanaugh focused on keeping me as his only friend from third grade on. He didn't ease up on me until after graduation, when I went off to college and he found himself in the town jail for drunk and disorderly after several days of drinking gin at the local bar and wrapping his ancient TransAm around a telephone pole on his way home.

"He wanted me to be his friend since the third grade," I told my parents. "And he never left me alone."

"He had issues," my mother said. "You probably were nicer to him than anyone."

"He was an idiot," I replied.

"You're not still down on him, are ya?" Dad asked. "It's been what? Twenty years?"

"Some things you just don't forget."

"The important thing," my mother said, "is that he's dead and you're not, and you still have a productive life ahead of you."

"How'd he die?"

"Somethin' about him leavin' a bar and gettin' slammed by a pickup truck." My father cleared his throat.

I wanted to laugh. It seemed fitting, an idiot like Cavanaugh dying after leaving a bar.

"He's buried out there behind the Presbyterian Church," Mom said.

10

"I take it ya won't be goin' out there to see the grave," Dad said.

"You take it right."

"You sound so *bitter*," Mom said.

"Just relieved."

"You're forty, dear. That all happened when you were a kid. You're not a kid no more."

"I'm thirty-nine, Mom…"

"Thirty-nine. Forty. What's the difference?"

"One really big, important number."

"How's your love life goin', by the way?" Dad asked.

Dad could be so embarrassing.

"Just fine."

"Whatever happened to that last one? The babe?"

"Maura?"

"Yup, that was her. Terrific. Sweet. Great legs."

"Andrew…" Mom did her best but couldn't do much about Dad once he started up.

Mom groaned. "Act your age, Andrew."

"Thought I was," he said.

"You're acting like…like…a—"

"A guy?"

"Yes. That."

"You oughta be used to that by now, Glenda. I mean, after forty-two years?"

"You'd think I would've had my head examined long before now, wouldn't ya?" she asked.

11

"Talk to you guys later." I picked up my wine glass. And thought about my childhood.

Bruce Cavanaugh was dead. It was amazing how little I cared. It was also amazing that a small part of me felt slighted because even though I had moved on with college and a solid career, I found that I might have considered my life more complete had I looked him up to let him know how well I'd been doing. I know how petty that sounded now, but I just couldn't help feeling this way.

The thing that should have bothered me but didn't was that someone I had known in high school was dead and I found that I didn't care one bit.

CHAPTER 2 - THE FIRST DAY

The next morning, instead of driving straight to my Orlando office on Robinson, I pulled into the cemetery behind the Presbyterian Church in Winter Park and eased down the winding gravel lane that would lead me to the grave where the *Sentinel* obit column had said Bruce Cavanaugh had been lain to rest.

I kept wondering why I was doing this in the first place. Did this strange impulse have something to do with doubt on my part? Did I need visible evidence that the Bruce was dead? Did I have to physically *see* the man's name etched into a stone marker to believe the issue was true? That I hadn't been lied to? That it had been nothing more than a cruel joke?

I kept thinking I was a moron. High school ended twenty years ago. No one remembered anything. Even the best of high school buddies split up not long after graduation to proceed with their individual lives. Did I honestly think I was so important in the life of some idiotic jerk I knew so long ago?

I stopped the car halfway down the path and spent the next five minutes scolding myself for coming here. Here I was, a thirty-nine-year-old businessman acting like a stupid kid jumping at shadows, driving to a cemetery early in the morning to verify that some irritating idiot from his past had been transported to the Great Beyond. I had to personally *see* the marker. And the name. And the dates. And the fact that there was actual *earth* covering the hole in the ground.

Put that way, I began wondering about my own sanity. I'd gone more than twenty years without giving Cavanaugh—or *any* of my former classmates—much thought. I'd gone through college, found gainful employment, met a lot of people, made contacts, endured half a dozen romances, then met and married a beautiful, demanding woman who left me after five turbulent years.

A normal existence, to be sure.

So why had things changed so drastically in the last twenty-four hours?

Was it Cavanaugh?

Or was it something else?

To be perfectly honest, the idiot had made quite a negative effect on my childhood. But that was in the past, and since I hadn't seen nor heard from him in so long, I couldn't very well consider our "relationship"—for want of a better term—something that had been essential in molding my personality. Cavanaugh had done absolutely nothing to permanently alter my character or change my destiny.

So why was I letting his memory postpone my daily activities just so I could take a quick peek at his gravestone?

Curiosity, obviously. Nothing more, nothing less. I needed to see for myself. I needed to personally look at the grave.

I needed to make absolutely certain the man was dead.

But why? Did I want to spit on the marker? Laugh at it? Speak some irreverent words to it? Piss on it? Stand on the mound of freshly shoveled dirt and tell him what a jerk he was?

It didn't matter. I had to see it before I did anything else. It was that simple.

I started moving the car again. Just two minutes later, I saw what looked like a fresh grave. I pulled up to the side of the gravel lane, stopped, put the car in park, flicked off the ignition, and got out. I walked up the short grassy incline leading to the marker.

Moments later, I saw it.

And when I did, my blood turned cold.

There it was, right in front of me:

Bruce Aaron Cavanaugh
1984-2022

I gazed helplessly at the marker, the grave, and the name, and thought of all those times the man now lying in the ground beneath my feet had irritated me beyond distraction. The many times he'd followed me down the hall. Told me to give him my homework to copy. Followed me to the rest room. Stood in front of the next urinal, sneaking a peek at me, making jokes. Whispered lewd suggestions to me in the classroom, when he caught me staring at one of the girls sitting in the next aisle. The times he'd tried to distract me by giggling or

15

whispering whenever I was called to the front of the room to give a book report. Those cursed times he called me on weekends to tell me he was coming over to hang out.

But right now, I realized that none of it mattered anymore because he was dead. His lifeless body was lying in the ground beneath my feet, decaying slowly into dust. Though he tried his best at every given opportunity to make my life miserable, I managed to overcome his efforts. It didn't matter that my marriage had crumbled; that aspect of my life had nothing to do with Cavanaugh. The fact that I had even graduated from high school was testament that I hadn't let anyone or anything from my childhood destroy me. I simply went on with my life.

"You couldn't do it," I whispered hotly to the marker. "You failed miserably. And I'm standing right here, staring in great satisfaction at the fresh dirt covering your miserable corpse."

That felt good, so I decided to go on. I even raised my voice—just in case his spirit hadn't heard me so far. "In fact, I'll bet I achieved more in the last couple of years than you managed in your entire worthless life."

A warm breeze swept down the hill. In that same instant, a coldness flowed through me, and I shivered.

What was *that*? My imagination? Or had something come up from the ground I was standing on?

You're being ridiculous.

Yes. I was. But to make sure, I moved off the fresh mound. Then, for the next few moments, I just stood there, gazing at the marker again. And waiting.

For what? For Cavanaugh's spirit to come out of the ground?

Silly? Yes. That sudden cold feeling had been nothing more than a product of my imagination. I was experiencing a plethora of emotions—triumph, guilt, self-satisfaction, a twinge of joy—and felt the need to exercise them all by standing on a dead man's grave.

What could be simpler?

However, that cold feeling rushed back just moments later, and the overwhelming urge to get the hell out of there consumed me. Without hesitation, I rushed down the grassy slope, where my car was parked.

I was on my way back to Orlando in just minutes.

***

After spending the workday worrying about my visit to the cemetery and cursing myself again and again for even going there, I got back to my apartment feeling more miserable than I've felt in a very long time.

I've been living by myself for the last six months. My wife Brittany dumped me after five years for greener pastures. In her case, the greener pastures turned out to be the first fabulously wealthy attorney who struck her fancy. She immediately moved on, leaving my life—as well as

17

my emotional state—in shambles. The details are no longer important. She chose a much more stable—and comfortable—future with one of Frisdale's most successful legal minds. Last I heard, she was living in splendor on her second husband's sixty-foot yacht, which docked frequently at Miami Beach, Key Largo, Biscayne Bay, and Bermuda.

To this day I remain at Frisdale's, manning my position as Reports Analyst in their Accounting Department, which I was doing when I met Brittany. My job is to look over their monthly financial reports. If I don't catch any errors or discrepancies, I pass them on to my supervisor. If I do find anything suspicious, I send it to the appropriate channel. If I miss something and my supervisor receives word of this from her supervisor, I get my wrist slapped. It's a high-paying job, but it's also monotonous and boring, and has caused burnout for countless others who have handled the position before me.

The fact that Brittany no longer works there somehow makes things worse, but I've learned to live with it. Frisdale's employs mostly females, making the scenery pleasant and rewarding, but also frustrating as hell. More than a third of the ladies working there are unattached, but after my fiasco with Brittany, I've been gun-shy and haven't had the desire to pursue anyone else.

But even though I discovered a tough inner core living within me that helped me survive our nasty divorce, another part of me wasn't strong enough to make it the rest of the way. My visits to

O'Malley's Bar, on the ground floor of the building I work in on Robinson, have become quite a bit longer than in the old days, when Brittany and I stopped off for a quick one before driving home to our Winter Park apartment. Back then, the stop-off translated into a vodka and tonic for me and a Tom Collins for her. For the next hour, we'd engage in mindless office chatter while the juke serenaded us with tunes from the eighties and nineties. Once the rush hour traffic had thinned, we would head on home.

Nowadays, my routine has morphed into two or three drinks before calling it a day. On other occasions, I have had five or six, but the business of calling a cab to take me home can be very expensive, so I usually stop at three, have supper at the Italian restaurant across the street, then drive home and fix myself three or four more before collapsing in bed.

It's not much of a life, but it's all mine, and who am I to quibble with needless unpleasant details?

At least, that was how I felt before.

But not tonight.

For some reason, my trip to the cemetery had done something strange and somewhat damaging to my psyche. I didn't know if it had something to do with the reality of seeing the marker, or that sudden gust of coldness that had nipped at me when my thoughts began running rampant. Whatever happened had freaked me out. I realized I was being silly and scolded myself, but that didn't seem to do the trick. Suddenly frustrated and anxious, I went to the kitchen cabinet, got out the vodka bottle, found a glass, and poured the first of what would be three strong drinks to calm me down.

But the fact remained: something strange had happened at that cemetery, and I had the strong feeling that I'd made a very bad mistake by going there.

CHAPTER 3 - THE SECOND DAY

After a very restless night, I got up sluggishly. The sun peeking in through the gap in the blinds registered, telling me it was daylight.

I squinted at my watch: 7:03. The pounding in my head had gradually diminished into a distant hum, clearing my mind.

My first question was: *What day is it?*

Thursday? Friday? Or was it Saturday?

In my advanced state of bewilderment, I just could not remember. All I recalled was that I made the mistake of driving to a cemetery the day after talking to my parents after dinner, and that I had gone to work that same day.

This told me that yesterday had to have been a weekday.

However, there were five of those to choose from, and since the vodka had turned everything into a throbbing blur, I found myself at a total loss. I had to somehow find out which day it was. I really needed to know if I was supposed to be in the office at nine o'clock.

Then it dawned on me. My cell phone had the time as well as the date.

I wasn't particularly fond of cell phones, but some of their software turned out to be amazingly useful. All I had to do was turn it on to find out the day.

Suddenly nervous, I dug into my jacket pocket, which hung from the chair, and fished it out. Then I

21

flicked it on. Once the light came on, it registered the time and date.

It was Friday.

Dammit. I had to go in this morning.

My heart raced. I had less than two hours to shower, shave, dress, slug down some coffee, choke down enough Aspirin to quell the throbbing in my head, and fight the morning traffic the six miles to the office.

***

Despite my severely impaired condition, I made it to the shower without stumbling or hitting my head on the sink or toilet. Gritting my teeth, I tried not to scream bloody murder as the icy flow cascaded down on my sensitive flesh.

Shivering beneath the cold spray, I squeezed my eyes shut. My fists were clenched, and my teeth chattered as the frosty blast plummeting down onto my skull brought me back to reality.

I remained immobile until I could take no more. Then, as my head finally cleared, I timidly reached out and added a little warm water to the glacier-like spray. It felt heavenly, so I added more.

A few minutes later, my blood pressure seemed to have settled back into a satisfying normalcy. I turned off the spray and, shaking, waited patiently for my circulation to trickle up into my head and hunt down some active brain cells. When I began to feel more alive and ready to rejoin the land of the living, I pulled the curtain aside and groped for the towel.

***

After drying off, I left the shower and timidly faced the mirror.

By this time, the pounding in my head had become less severe. My vision had cleared up somewhat, and as I stared at the clueless idiot in the mirror, I decided to forgo shaving for one day. Thankfully, my red-brown stubble was sparse and not very noticeable. Besides, I didn't trust my trembling hand to handle a triple-bladed razor without botching things up by slicing and dicing favorite portions of my face. It was all I could do to aim the blow dryer at my head and direct the hot blast at my wet skull.

Once my hair was dry, then arranged in a semblance of acceptable neatness with the help of a comb, I went back into the bedroom and set about going through the painful process of putting on fresh clothes.

Ten exhausting minutes later, I began to feel reasonably alive again and decided to make a cup of coffee. It wasn't quite 8:00. I usually left the condo at 8:20, so I had twenty minutes before driving to work. A cup of hot coffee and a quick breakfast of buttered toast and three Aspirin would hopefully help me get through the morning.

I left the bedroom and went down the hall. I began thinking of the previous day and cursed myself once again for driving to the cemetery. And, of course, for drinking so much when I got back home. I couldn't think of any sensible reason for having done such stupid things in the first place. The trip to the cemetery was bad enough, but the excessive vodka told me that I needed to have my head examined. There was no reason in the world why I should have wasted my time visiting the marker of the worthless idiot who had tormented me during my childhood.

Had I been looking for closure? Or was it satisfaction?

No matter what the reason, the trip to the gravestone had been a complete waste of time.

And as for the heavy drinking back at the apartment...

I knew damned well that my liver was cursing me up and down. I'd be turning forty in just a couple of months and should start taking better care of myself. It was unhealthy and extremely dangerous to continue doing the same mindless things I'd done before graduating from college. I had the rest of my life to look forward to and didn't want to spend it dead, crippled, or hooked up to machines.

Once I'd finished scolding myself for my indiscretions, I decided to concentrate on the day ahead. I was about to step into the kitchen when I stopped cold in the doorway.

I had the strangest feeling someone else was in the room.

***

Something cold and gooey crawled up my throat.

It took all my willpower to force it back down so I could speak. It didn't matter what my eyes—or my mind—was telling me. I had to come to grips

24

with the fact that after visiting the grave of a man I hadn't seen in the last twenty years, I was now standing in my kitchen, sensing the presence of someone or something.

Just then, I heard a soft voice and an irritating chuckle. "How goes it, Frankie-Boy?"

The voice—as well as the chuckle—sounded like it had come from the direction of the kitchen window.

I closed my gaping mouth and struggled to get my thoughts in order. When I started talking again, I tried a simple sentence and hoped it would come out. Baby steps, as the saying went. "W-Who's there?"

"Guess!"

After swallowing that cold, gooey lump, I took a deep breath and tried very hard not to panic. "Bruce?"

"Right on the button!"

"B-But..."

"But what?"

He obviously had no idea what I was going to say, so I came right out and said it. "You're...*dead*..."

A pause. "Yep, you sure do pick up on just about everything, my main man!"

This was making less and less sense. "But you're *dead*!"

"Yeah. We've already been through that one. Guess what? I kinda got that same vibe myself when I woke up in that box, so let's move on to somethin' else, all righty?"

I had no idea what to say, so I didn't say anything. I was still trying very hard to accept what was happening, but it just didn't make any sense. The man was dead, but I could hear his voice. And it had to be Cavanaugh. He'd addressed me by name.

Still, this couldn't be happening. It couldn't be happening because the man was dead.

"Frankie?"

"Dead. You're dead."

"Yeah, I already got that. You havin' trouble with this, by any chance? You keep sayin' it like ya don't really believe it."

"I don't know if I do."

And I didn't—not really. Although I knew nothing about death, I believed that when a person died, he or she turned into a spirit and drifted quietly away, most likely into what I only know as the spirit world. At least, that sounded like what would happen if that religious belief in death and the afterlife had any credence.

"Look at me, Frankie. Do I *look* dead?"

"I can't *see* you, Bruce..."

A pause. "Yep, you're right. I can't see me, neither. This spirit crap sure has its ups and downs. Bummer, ain't it?"

"It makes me wonder if you're even there."

"You're *talkin'* to me, ain't ya?"

"I hear your *voice*..."

"You're lookin' at me, right?"

"My eyes are pointed at the area where I think your voice is coming from, but—"

26

"But *what*?"

"You're *dead*…" There was just no other way of assessing this.

A chuckle. "Yeah, I was right. You just can't get your tiny mind wrapped around that one, can ya?"

"Listen. I saw your marker. Your grave."

"Yeah, I picked up on that vibe, too. Didn't know who you were at first, but then I kinda caught a peek. Then I remembered. If I hadn't been dead, I woulda crapped my pants. Imagine that. My old buddy Frankie-Boy Langley, comin' all the way across town just to see little ol' me. You coulda slapped me senseless with a silly stick!"

"You've got a grave. With your name on it."

"No shit? Ya mean, one of those *stony* things? At a *cemetery*?"

I knew he was making fun of me, but I nodded anyway.

"How 'bout that? A stony thing. At a cemetery. What'll they think of next?"

"A body that stays dead, maybe?" His arrogance was annoying me.

"Good one, Frankie-Boy. By the way, you said some pretty nasty things back there."

"Where?" I knew exactly what he meant; I just wanted to hear him say it.

"Where else? The cemetery, doofus."

"The words came right from the heart."

"Ouch. Seems like you got a tad bitter in your old age. When was the last time you got laid, my friend?"

27

"This isn't happening." I figured that if I kept saying that, my subconscious would eventually kick in and make the rest of me believe it as well.

"What isn't happening, Frankie?"

"You're dead, Bruce."

"Frankie, I don't know if somethin' rattled loose in that head of yours, but the way it looks to me? You're beginnin' to sound just a tad monotonous."

"You really shouldn't be here, you know."

"And where should I be, my main man?"

"Somewhere else."

"I guess I decided to make a special visit here, didn't I?"

"How'd you do it?"

"Wish I could tell ya, but I can't say that I recall much. You just gave off some vibes and I picked up on 'em. Then I guess I just followed 'em and ended up here, in your pad. Nice pad, by the way. Small, but roomy enough if ya bring home a babe to get laid."

"Why?"

"Why what?"

"Why are you here?"

"We're buds, Frankie—remember?"

"I haven't seen you in twenty years."

"Don't matter none. Buds stay buds, don't they?"

His statement really angered me. "We weren't exactly *buds*..."

"No?"

"Hell, no."

28

"We spent a shitload of time together in the day. "

I couldn't believe this idiot said something like that.

"Nothin' to say?"

"Nothing you'll like to hear..."

"Spill the beans, Frankie-Boy. Give it up. C'mon, now...let 'er loose!"

"You sat beside me in the seventh grade so you could copy my test answers. You called me on weekends to ask if you could come over and hang out, and when I didn't answer the phone, you showed up anyway, even when we had company. You played dirty tricks on me and blamed it on other kids, and when I found out it was you, you just laughed and slapped me on the shoulder. Time together? Yes, but the time we spent together anything but good. And no. Just in case you haven't guessed by now, we weren't *chums*."

I could imagine him grinning that disgusting crooked grin that I'd hated so much in those days. "We were buds, Frankie. Admit it."

"We weren't buds at all. In fact, you were probably the most irritating jerk I ever knew."

"C'mon, Frankie. Let it out. You *liked* me hangin' around."

"I *hated* you hanging around. I spent entirely too much time trying to avoid you, but you always showed up. And at the most inconvenient times."

He didn't reply to that.

The resulting silence instantly grew uncomfortable.

29

"How'd you die?" I decided it was time to get off that unpleasant subject before I got even angrier.

More silence. He was no doubt thinking it over.

"Last thing I remember, I'd had a few and left the bar. Then I believe I just blacked out and began sleepin' it off. Then as I said before, I heard ya talkin' at me, and when I woke up, I saw ya up there, lookin' down at me and sayin' some really bad things. I musta fallen asleep again, and when I woke up, you were gone. But as I also said, I kinda sniffed you out and it brought me right here."

"Just like that?"

"I guess so…"

I shook my head.

"Think I'm lyin'?"

"I really have no idea."

"*You* got any ideas how the fuck I got here when I woke up after sleepin' it off?"

"All I know is, you're dead."

"You sound like you're really losin' it, ol' chum. What's wrong? Maybe that little pot you've got goin' on has done somethin' to your head. What happened? Too many steaks and potatoes? Looks like a beer gut to me…"

I was getting even angrier, but when I thought of the situation, I realized there was no reason for it. He was dead—he shouldn't be able to irritate me anymore.

Or maybe he wasn't really here…

My heavy drinking was obviously responsible for all this. This wasn't even happening. I was no

30

doubt hallucinating. My trip to the cemetery had influenced all this.

The only thing that made any sense was that I was coming down from my hangover. That had to be the reason. Since I was settling down and beginning to relax, my brain might have arrived at a very vulnerable point, and what I was hearing was something my subconscious snatched up from my trip to the cemetery and turned into total nonsense.

I closed my eyes and told myself that when I opened them again, the voice communicating with me would be gone.

After about ten seconds, I decided to open them and—

"Frankie? You takin' a nap? That ain't polite, ya know, dozin' off when you got company…"

The voice still hadn't gone.

However, it sounded hazier than before.

Hazier…

Yes. Though the voice hadn't *gone*, it had suddenly become less distinct. Less *there*. This told me—

"You're awfully quiet. What's…on…ain't hap…me…"

"Your voice…"

"Yeah?"

"It's fading."

"Howza…"

"You're fading. Vanishing. Getting ready to disappear."

"Son of a…what's goin'…what…fuck—"

31

"You're fading." My voice had grown stronger. I felt less queasy, more confident. Perhaps this was because I no longer thought I was going crazy or hallucinating. The fact that he was slipping away told me he wasn't a hallucination at all. He was a spirit. And he was now going back to some other place, where he belonged.

"What's hap...why...fuck...why can't...*feel* any—"

"It's very simple."

"Tell... What's goin'... Dammit!" Panic had taken over. "*Tell* me!"

"Like I just said, it's very simple. You're fading because you're dead. No longer living. Deceased. Ashes to ashes. Dust to dust. Worm food, to be more precise."

"I *can't* be...*can't*..."

A loud groan. When he spoke again, his voice sounded muffled, distant—as if he were talking from some faraway place. "I *can't* be... If I...dead...then...I couldn't..."

Silence.

I remained standing there for several minutes, tensely waiting.

After another five minutes or so, I began breathing normally again. It took me a few more minutes to accept what I'd just experienced, and I wondered once again if I'd been hallucinating. After all, people couldn't come back from the dead and pay you a visit in your kitchen, could they?

I had to believe that. Otherwise, I might just as well commit myself to the first mental institution I could find.

Bruce Cavanaugh was dead. I saw the marker, the grave.

So why should I believe that his spirit had come to visit me in my kitchen?

He hadn't been here at all. It was that simple. The vodka had messed up my mind. I had to believe that. I truly did.

Then, as all this reasoning brought me back to cold reality, I remembered what I'd been doing before this weird, unexplained event happened. *Work. Get there. Now...*

Forcing down the panic, I rushed out of the kitchen.

***

The twenty-minute drive to downtown Orlando turned out to be strangely enjoyable.

I suppose it was because I felt genuine relief— as well as a bizarre sense of peace—after that frightening episode in my condo. The more I drove, the safer and less stressed I felt. But even so, I couldn't wrap my mind around the fact that a spirit from my past had somehow communicated with me in my kitchen.

Why would a man I hadn't seen in twenty years come back from the dead and visit *me*, of all people? Was it just because of my brief visit to his grave? Other than my countless unpleasant encounters with him during my school years, I hadn't known Cavanaugh at all—nor did I *want* to.

33

The only breaks from his annoyances I can remember in those days happened when he didn't show up for class. Since he hated school, his absences had been frequent, but not nearly often enough.

Maybe the key to all this hinged on what he'd told me—that his spirit had somehow sensed my presence. It sounded far-fetched, but I couldn't come up with anything else. And it was no wonder. Reality had literally vanished from my consciousness not long after I came home, had the vodka, and decided to sleep it off.

It was bad enough to struggle through a bad hangover, but far worse to engage in a conversation with a dead man while fighting off the hangover.

Reality, thank God, intervened the moment I reached the parking garage on Robinson and went up the ramp, turning my earlier hallucination into an unpleasant memory.

Ed Gottman, one of the three CPAs at Frisdale's, slid his bulky frame from the front seat of his maroon SUV and waddled over as I made my way to the elevators. "Rough night, Langley?" he asked in his loud, unpleasant baritone voice.

Without replying, I pressed the *down* button and waited. Gottman was a damned good CPA, but hardly a people person. I didn't know anyone at the company who liked the man.

"No offense, but you look like shit."

"Thanks." I decided not to say too much. I really didn't feel like talking. My head hurt, and I found that I couldn't stop obsessing about the kitchen incident.

Gottman continued his irritating inspection. "Decide to pass on a clean shave this morning?"

I wasn't in the mood for this and hoped it wouldn't take much to stop it. "I decided that a *dirty* shave might not go so well with this outfit," I replied with a glare.

Instead of replying, he consulted his wristwatch and fiddled with his French cuff.

We rode down the rest of the way in tense silence.

As I continued obsessing about Cavanaugh, I thought for a moment that I had some sort of explanation, but as soon as I tried focusing on it, the same message came up. The message was short and to the point. It said: *a man you once knew in high school died, came back from the dead, and visited you in your kitchen…*

That was what it amounted to. And no matter how I tried to analyze it, it made no sense. And to make matters even more complicated, something else came to me that didn't exactly give me a warm fuzzy.

Somehow, I have to deal with this...

But how could I possibly deal with something I didn't believe happened in the first place? How could I understand something that defied all logic? Cavanaugh was dead. How could I convince myself that he'd come back from the dead, then paid me a surprise visit in my kitchen?

I didn't believe in ghosts and never thought it possible for the dead to come back and appear. I wasn't even totally positive about what I'd heard in the kitchen.

Would this same thing happen *again*?

Was this something that normally didn't happen at all? A glitch in the universe, perhaps? A slight tear in the fabric of time? An accidental tangling between two worlds?

Most important of all…should I worry about it?

"I will *not* worry about this," I told myself as I shuffled down the carpeted hall. "And I certainly won't let it bother me. I can't. I just can't."

"What was that, Frank?"

I spun around.

Alexandria Sommers, Frisdale's receptionist, stood in the doorway of the lunchroom just a few feet behind me, watching me. As always, her thick black hair spilled over one shoulder, much of it curling over the top of her large right breast. Her sleeveless cream-colored blouse displayed her slim, well-toned, deeply tanned figure. Her black skirt, reaching just two inches below the knee, as well as her open-toed black sandals with three-inch spikes, accentuated her shapely legs. She held a thick manila envelope in the crook of her left arm. Her large dark eyes settled on me.

"Just talking to myself." I forced a grin, but I knew she could tell I was uncomfortable.

She smiled back and lowered her voice. "You did remember the weekly budget meeting scheduled for this afternoon, didn't you?"

36

Shit. This was Friday. All members of the company attended a budget meeting every Friday. I'd been working here for nine years and knew that very well. However, I found it strange that the notion of it hadn't even entered my mind.

It was undoubtedly because of Cavanaugh. Otherwise, my brain wouldn't have been so fragmented, and I certainly would have remembered.

The hangover had disoriented my brain activity more than I had imagined.

"Of course." I forced myself to keep smiling. I didn't want to tell her that a dead man had visited me in my condo half an hour earlier. That would have probably sent her directly to Frisdale, asking him to talk to me to see if I needed to talk to the company psychiatrist.

Alex gave me one of her gentle smiles. "Just to refresh your memory, Mr. Belknap from our Miami branch will also be there. He said he might be running a little late, but in case he isn't, the meeting's still set for one."

Her smile, plus the way she was staring at my face, told me she was hinting that I should grab a quick shave and give myself a careful once-over. Alex was a sharp lady and didn't miss much. She could obviously see that the knot of my tie wasn't right and that I hadn't properly buttoned my jacket. Alex was also very classy. She knew how to motivate a guy without making him aware of what she was doing.

I nodded and smiled. "Thanks, Alex."

37

She winked. Then she turned, sashaying down the hall in her sexy, hip-swaying walk, which had, on many occasion, halted all conversation and other forms of office activity involving the males and many of the females. In other circumstances, I would have continued standing there, watching her, and trying my best not to drool. But this morning, there were more important issues than watching how great those legs looked moving beneath that perfect ass.

I slipped into my cube, opened my desk drawer, and grabbed my Aspirin bottle. Hoping I wouldn't tear up my stomach by adding to what I had taken earlier, I dry-swallowed three to help eliminate what was left of the throbbing in my head. Then I yanked open the bottom drawer and snatched up my emergency tune-up kit, which contained my comb, brush, toothbrush, toothpaste, deodorant stick, electric razor, and cologne. I didn't waste another moment as I rushed out of the office and headed directly to the bathroom down the hall.

***

The first half-hour of the meeting went without incident.

Old Man Frisdale—as well as his Executive Director, Calvin Ross—gave me their usual look of condescension as I shuffled into the conference room and took my seat as close to the heavily-tinted window as I dared. Since they gave everyone else the same disdainful look each time we attended a meeting, I didn't take offense. In fact, I had nothing to feel self-conscious about. Just hours earlier, I had splashed my face with cold water, shaved, applied cologne, combed my hair, and spent considerable time reworking the knot of my tie. In the end, I appeared just as neat and professional as everyone else.

However, despite the overhaul, six cups of black coffee and three more Aspirin, I found that I was just as exhausted and as stressed as I had been before driving to work. Although several hours had passed since my bizarre experience in my kitchen, the event continued to plague me, and I quickly discovered that I couldn't get any work done at all after returning to my desk. I just hoped that the meeting would help occupy my mind with other issues.

Frisdale started off with his usual long-winded rhetoric about the company's place in the future of Corporate America, and after nearly twenty boring minutes, Ross made his weekly announcements regarding the company's scheduled activities.

Ronald Belknap, our Miami associate, had only been thirty-five minutes late. The moment he came in, he took over for the next twenty-five minutes, reading from his notes and giving his personal take on what our company needed to do to stay streamlined, fit, and competitive.

I sat stiffly in my seat and struggled to give everyone the impression that I was reading the goals Frisdale had drafted and handed out before the meeting. In fact, I was fighting to stay awake. The pounding in my head, softened minimally by the Aspirin, had eased into a gentle cloudiness, and while my irritating headache prevented me from nodding off, I found early on that I couldn't keep my mind on anything that was said.

Then, without warning, I sensed something strange.

My first reaction was that Cavanaugh's spirit had returned. Although I could not make out an actual vision, I could see some sort of faint gray blur appear directly behind Old Man Frisdale.

I sat bolt upright in my chair. The papers dropped from my grasp and slid lazily in a wavy, zigzag pattern across the table. Two pages dropped to the floor, but I found that I couldn't move. The only thing that existed at that moment was the blurred image of what was most likely Bruce Cavanaugh hovering near my boss. And judging by everyone else's total lack of reaction, I realized that I was the only one in the room who could see it.

"Langley?" Frowning, Frisdale was watching me closely. "Everything all right?"

I tried to reply, but a cold lump had developed in my throat, preventing me from speaking. All I could do was nod.

He blinked behind his thick glasses. "Something you'd like to add?"

I swallowed the lump and eventually recovered some feeling in my throat. "S-Sir?"

"Something was obviously said that you'd like to comment on. We all would very much like to hear what you have to say."

"Go, Frankie-boy," Cavanaugh's voice urged, chuckling. "This is bound to be knee-slappin' entertainment as well as downright top-notch fascinating! Let's get on with your shtick."

Suddenly, Cavanaugh's spirit had become the only thing in the room that existed in my world. My anger took over and without thinking, I lashed out. "What the...what do you think you're doing here?"

"I beg your pardon?" Frisdale tilted his bald head. It was only then that I realized I'd spoken aloud to a spirit, and in front of twenty people who were *not* spirits. In one single, terrifying moment, twenty pairs of eyes were staring intensely at me.

"How long's your boss-man been bald?" Cavanaugh was chuckling again.

"Sorry, sir..." I fought hard to focus on the old man and struggled to think of a way out of this. "I was just...thinking out loud."

"He sure has bundles and bundles of gunky gray hair sticking out of his ears..." Cavanaugh sounded serious. "You could knit a sweater with it." A short pause. "He's got some icky wax buildup in there, too."

I wanted to tell him to get the hell out of here but could only imagine what that would have done.

"About what?" Frisdale seemed oddly interested.

"He's also got a bunch of funny-lookin' moles over here." Cavanaugh's voice hadn't strayed from his position behind Frisdale. "I'll bet if we connected them, we could come up with a cartoon character. A baby roach...or maybe a mouse..."

I rubbed my eyes and realized that I was most likely going insane.

"Got a magic marker on ya, Frankie-boy?"

"Langley? You all right?"

"I think…I need some air, sir."

"You're not sick, are you?"

"No, sir…"

Frisdale's face instantly squeezed into a giant knuckle. "You don't look at all too well."

The people flanking me immediately inched their chairs away from me.

"I think I might be catching…the bug…"

"Then go home, dammit." Frisdale's face was still covered in wrinkles. "You know damned well that I hate my people coming in sick and infecting the company. Everyone working here should know my policy by now."

"Yes, sir…"

"I'm sure you've got sick time coming."

"Yes, sir."

"Go home, Langley."

"Yes, sir."

"*Now.*"

"Damn nifty idea," Cavanaugh agreed, sounding solemn. "If I wasn't already dead, I'd worry about picking up somethin' from you, Frankie. You really should be a tad more considerate, ya know."

I struggled to keep from glaring.

"Your eyes look blood-shot, Frankie-boy." Cavanaugh's voice sounded closer. "And I'm not sure I like the looks of that vein that's sticking out of your—"

"*Now*, Langley!" Frisdale's voice had grown much louder.

I got up and ran out of the room.

***

Before leaving the building, I stopped by the water cooler and swallowed two more Aspirin.

Alex Sommers sat at her desk, watching me as she put down her phone. "You don't look well, Frank. Flu?"

"Maybe." I figured being vague would be the best way to go.

"Whoa! Holy shit, man!" Cavanaugh's voice was uncomfortably close. He was obviously checking her out. Alex's crossed legs, revealed by the short skirt, would do a number on anyone. I'd never figured that she could frustrate a dead man. But she was doing just that.

I wanted to tell him to ease off but knew that would be a big mistake. Instead, I told Alex I was leaving early.

She nodded. "Good idea. Go straight home and climb into bed."

"Um, you wouldn't consider joinin' us, would ya, babe?" Cavanaugh's chuckle revolted me. "I don't have what you'd call an actual *body* anymore, but I can still watch. How 'bout you and Frankie-boy, here, get with it and do your best tryin' to hide that banana! Wow! Those titties are turnin' on a dead man!"

"Stop it." I couldn't help it. My anger had taken over again.

"Pardon me?" Alex's large dark eyes had drifted over.

"Uh...just yelling at this pesky little ache in my side." I hurried out of there before Cavanaugh could coax me into making even more of an ass of myself.

"Hurry up, dammit." The location of his voice suggested that he had moved closer to the elevator doors.

I suspected that he would only perform his perverted shtick if I was right there. I could tell by his smartass remarks and irritating chuckling that he really enjoyed watching me embarrass myself.

He was humiliating me just as effectively as a spirit as he had done twenty years earlier, as a mortal.

"Is *that* what I am?" he asked, sounding hurt. "A pesky little *ache*?"

"Why *me*?" I asked. "Why pick on *me*?"

"Frankie-boy, I'm not *pickin'* on you..."

"What the hell would you call it, then?"

"Havin' a little funzies with an old chum?"

"As I already told you, I was *never* your old *chum*..."

"Then why'd you come and visit me? No one else did. I find that very...well, touching."

"I went to your grave to see if it was actually *true*." I scanned the hall before saying anything else. Luckily, we were alone. "I didn't honestly believe you were dead and wanted to make sure. Personally, I thought you were too nasty to die. But when I saw your marker, I realized you were dead and no longer tormenting anyone. It really moved me and made me believe that there might actually be an order to the Universe. But since you've obviously come back from the dead just to torment me, I'm beginning to think differently…"

"You really think I'm *tormentin'* you?"

"What do *you* call it?"

"Checkin' up on an old friend."

I scanned the area once again. No one was within earshot.

"To repeat myself, we're not *friends*, dammit. I didn't even *know* you and never *wanted* to. You were the school nuisance, and you stuck to me and irritated me for more years than I care to remember. And, by the way, you're not *checking up on* me, you're *tormenting* me—and in front of my boss and everyone else I work with."

He didn't reply.

I faced the elevator doors, hoping he'd just disappear again.

After more than a minute of silence, I thought my hopes had been answered. Then his irritating voice came back: "Ya do look sick, ya know."

"Listen to me," I whispered. "I don't know what you're trying to do, but—"

I stopped when one of the secretaries from Payroll walked over to wait for the elevator beside me.

"Hi, Frank."

"Lois…"

"How ya doing? You look under the weather."

"I haven't been feeling well lately."

Her brows pushed together. "Really? That's too bad."

"This one's a *real* cutie." Judging by the location of his voice, I figured Cavanaugh had moved closer to her. "Why the hell didn't ya tell me you worked with so many sweet babes?"

I glared before realizing it.

Lois caught it. "Something wrong?"

"Everything's just fine." I put a hand over my gut. "Just a little heartburn."

"Really?" She opened her bag. "I think I might have something for that…"

"Maybe she's got a twelve-pack of rubbers in there for ya, Frankie-boy…"

I ignored him. "I'm okay. Thanks anyway."

She stopped rummaging. "You sure?"

I nodded.

Lois snapped her bag shut.

"How 'bout pullin' up that annoying skirt so Frankie-boy can get in there, pull those yummy thighs apart, and pull off a seriously heavy-duty probe?"

The elevator doors opened.

I followed Lois into the empty car. Two other women rushed in just before the doors closed.

I could tell Cavanaugh was looking everyone up and down.

I wanted to strangle him.

"This one smells pretty good, Frankie-boy. I think she might be givin' off some of those sex-hormone thingys."

I closed my eyes and tried to breathe normally.

46

"I don't know what the hell else they call it. Babes do it all the time. It gets a guy horny even if the babe's ten feet away. She just points her face atcha and you go all stiff and hot. Mostly stiff. My ex-wife Mona did it to me from the time she woke up in the morning till the time she fell asleep at night. All she had to do was look at me and I went totally apeshit—"

"Pheromones," I said without thinking.

"That's it! Fuckin' pheromones! That's the shit that comes outa your nose and gets 'em all hot and bothered without ya havin' to do anything else!"

Lois backed up until her fleshy butt pressed against the doors. The other two women backed up as well. The other lady gawked at me as if she'd just smelled something disgusting.

"Just thinking to myself," I stammered. "I've...got a lot on my mind..."

The car stopped. The elevator doors hummed open.

All three women bolted out of the car.

**

My nerves made me shake as I hurried down the hall.

Although he hadn't said anything, I was certain Cavanaugh remained close. No one passed, so at least I didn't have to worry about anyone hearing me if I did say anything to him.

I decided to ignore him while focusing on the metal door awaiting me straight ahead, but soon found that to be impossible. Even though he was a spirit and impossible to see, it was difficult to keep from looking around for him.

"C'mon, Frankie... You can't stay pissed at me forever, can ya?"

I continued staring at the door.

"*You* were the one blurted out that shit in the elevator, ya know..."

I still didn't speak.

He chuckled. "Ya can't blame a guy, can ya? I couldn't help myself. That babe's prob'ly *way* the hell on the wrong side of forty, but she still looked good and was sendin' out all kinds of signals. Ya know what? I'll bet she'd even put out if you went back and told her she was turnin' you on. Ya know, all those juicy pheromones drippin' out of her nostrils would really make this a humdinger of a—"

"Leave me alone."

"Listen—"

"I said—"

"C'mon, Frankie-boy...can'tcha take a joke? Twenty years from now, if you're still alive and kickin', I'll bet you'll have a good chuckle over all this. And ya know what else?"

"I don't want to *hear* anything else. Not from *you*."

"I'll prob'ly be able to get ya all the pussy you could ever want."

"Now why would you want to do something like that?"

"Hmmm... I dunno... Maybe 'cause of what I used to do to irritate ya in school."

48

I couldn't believe what he just said. "You mean you actually feel *badly* about what you did to me back then?"

He didn't reply. Then he snickered and said, "Naw. Not really."

"I didn't think so."

"How'd ya know?"

"You're an idiot."

"Wow… Don't sugarcoat it, now…"

"I really mean it. You were one of those kids who can't help being irritating, and you seemed to be obsessed with latching onto someone just as a tick would cling to a dog. Idiots like you aren't known to be sympathetic. You couldn't find a shred of decency anywhere in your bones if your life depended on it."

"Ouch. Where'd *that* come from?"

"Maybe from all those many times you latched onto me like a leech and wouldn't leave me alone."

Another shrug. "Aw, c'mon now, Frankie-boy. Let bygones be bygones."

"That's easy for *you* to say."

"Listen. Lemme find ya some top-grade pussy. You'll feel better once ya get laid."

I didn't reply. I hoped that by being silent, he'd vanish and leave me in peace.

"Ya wanna know how I can do it?"

"No."

"Here's how."

"I just said—"

"You asked me about the Afterlife, right? Well, I'm tryin' to explain what happened and what I can do for ya."

Once again, I didn't reply, but I could tell he was going to talk no matter what. I sincerely hoped that he'd run out of ectoplasm once again and disappear. I needed a break from him—even if only for a few minutes.

"See, I just found out that I'm dead—right? Anyway, I also found out that dead guys can do a shitload of nifty things once they learn how to direct their energies the right way. Wanna know what I can do?"

"No."

"I can do things with my head that I couldn't do before. I can make things happen. All I gotta do is think about somethin' for a few seconds. Then it happens. Doesn't that sound cool?"

"Yeah. Real cool." The elevator didn't seem to be getting any closer.

"That was kinda sarcastic, wasn't it, Frankie-boy?"

"Go back where you belong. Leave me the hell alone."

"I was just there. It's no fun, dude. *This* is where it's at."

"Isn't anyone else back there? Someone you can talk to? Someone else you can torment? Someone other than me?"

"A whole buncha folks, but they're all workin' their own shtick. Some of 'em, they're just wanderin' around, lookin' for folks they used to know. It's really depressing and kinda boring. But the others?" He snickered. "*They're* the ones having a *real* blast."

I finally reached the elevator. A minute later, the door slid open. It was empty, thank God.

As the door closed behind me, I couldn't believe my good luck. I could tell I was alone in the car. All alone. Just me. No one else. Then I listened. Nothing but the grinding whine of the car going up.

Had his ectoplasm finally run out? How much of a supply did he have? How much did any of them have?

It probably wasn't an unlimited amount. Judging by what he'd done during the last half-hour, I guessed that he had probably exhausted his supply had before running low or zapping the source completely.

How long would this peace and quiet last?

I decided to time my sudden reprieve before I got out of the elevator.

I checked my watch. So far, it was about thirty seconds since I'd seen him. I'd be getting out in another half-minute. That would make it a full minute without his annoying intrusion.

The door opened. I stepped out.

So far, so good.

Relieved, I took a deep breath and began walking briskly down the aisle.

Then, just as I was about to turn into my space, I heard his cursed voice once again: "Miss me?"

51

The location of the voice suggested Cavanaugh was standing between my car and the one parked next to mine.

I really hated him for being dead at that moment. If he had been a mortal, I would have snuck up behind him and pushed him over the concrete wall.

I suddenly wished I could make myself invisible. Then I could slip past him, get in my car, and leave before he realized what happened.

The moment I drew closer, he said, "C'mere, Frankie-boy. C'mon over here, have a gander at this."

I had no choice. To get in my car, I had to move through him. Like it or not, I had to do as he said.

I walked over to the wall and looked down at the street, where an elderly woman with a cane was crossing at the intersection.

"See 'er?"

"Of course I see her. I'm standing right here. If *you* can see her, so can I…"

"Wow, what an attitude…"

"I wonder who gave it to me…"

"Just hold your water for a minute and check this out."

The woman started crossing. As soon as she'd gone ten steps, a sports car sped down the street in her direction.

My heart skipped a beat. "She's gonna be hit!"

Cavanaugh didn't reply.

I yelled at her, but the traffic sounds drowned me out. Horrified, I turned away. I didn't want to watch.

"Keep watchin', Frankie."

"I can't!"

"Trust me."

I glared. "Why the hell should I?"

"You'll be sorry if ya don't…"

Despite my instincts, I turned back to the street and held my breath. The car didn't slow down or swerve, but still managed to miss the woman by inches.

"How the hell…what the…what did he…that car…she should've been hit!"

Cavanaugh chuckled. "I guess ya can't see the old dude walkin' beside her."

I gawked at the lady as she reached the other side of the street. I didn't see anyone near her. "She's alone."

"*Is* she?"

I kept looking but still didn't see anyone.

"She's got someone right there beside her."

I scanned the area around her but still didn't see anyone else in the picture. "I don't…I can't see *anyone*…"

"That's 'cause the dude beside her is dead."

"You mean—"

"*I* can see her…"

"*You* can see someone *else* there?"

"I'm dead, too, remember?"

"But the car… It didn't swerve. At all…"

53

"Don't matter. She's got her old man walkin' beside her. He's her angel."

Despite my anger, my confusion, this somehow made sense. "He *died*...and became her *angel*?"

"Yep."

"And *that's* why she isn't dead right now?"

"Frankie-boy, you sure are one quick study!"

I was so amazed at this that I didn't take issue with his sarcasm. "That was...incredible."

"Know what else is incredible, Frankie-boy?"

I was afraid to ask. "What?"

Cavanaugh laughed. "Guess..."

"I'm really not in the mood to—"

A chuckle. "Don't drop a load, now, but I'm pretty damn sure I'm *your* angel!"

***

My tightly clenched fists no longer felt the steering wheel as I drove through the heavy Orlando afternoon traffic.

Cavanaugh had vanished just moments after delivering his appalling message, giving me all the time in the world to digest the full meaning of what he had just said.

Alone-time, especially right now, turned out to be just what the doctor ordered. I didn't want him around. What he just told me was too much. I needed time to accept the possibility that if he was not just being a smartass, I now had my very own personal "angel" hovering around me, and this "angel" was the same asshole who had made my childhood a living hell.

No. I *wouldn't* accept this. I couldn't. I didn't *deserve* it.

I wasn't a bad person. I knew I wasn't perfect, but no one else was, either. I was polite and well-mannered. I opened the door for people and apologized to them even when I really didn't have to. I had never treated anyone with less respect than I would want in return.

So why did I have to face the fact that the same jerk who had taunted me during my childhood would become my guardian angel for the rest of my life?

Was this some misdirected Karma that had tracked me down to punish me for something I did that I couldn't even remember?

Had someone in my past hexed me for something they blamed me for?

Had some gypsy put a curse on me by mistake?

I stopped at a red light on Colonial and struggled to remember any and all ills I'd inflicted during my life—who I'd wronged, who I'd hurt. I had been in the workforce more than twenty years but hadn't hurt or stepped on anyone in the process. I dated, of course, but I had never been a player and never cheated on a woman. I was always the one who received the Dear John letter. And to be clear, I had never sent one of those in my entire life.

I just could not think of anything I'd ever done that would explain why someone as infuriating as Bruce Cavanaugh would reach beyond the grave and mark me as his personal property. All I did was visit the man's tombstone, for God's sake. I did it only for the sake of curiosity. To see if what I had heard was true—that he was truly dead. I had no ulterior motive and certainly didn't derive any pleasure or amusement from standing on that plot of freshly dug earth. I had said a few unpleasant things, but since the man was dead and no longer aware of anything, I didn't think what I'd said would really hurt or cause harm to anyone else.

However, fate chose, for some reason, to bring him back to the land of the living with the single purpose of tormenting *me,* of all the people in the world.

"Why me?" I yelled to myself. "What gives that idiot the right to—"

The honking of the vehicle behind me told me the light had changed.

With a deep sigh, I pulled my foot off the brake and proceeded through the intersection.

As I drove down the street, I focused on the subject of death and the hereafter.

How was it even possible for something like this to happen?

I always figured that when you died, you were dead. If I really did believe in the spirit thing, in which I constantly had doubts, I would deem it only logical that the spirit left the mortal world and moved on to a different dimension. Religious people believed in the soul issue, with the good drifting up into the light and the bad suffering in darkness. There was, of course, the ghost thing that had been a great source of debate for centuries, some saying they had seen evidence of spirits, while skeptics and scientists stubbornly maintained the opposite view.

But the idea of someone coming back from the dead? To torment me? Then informing me that he had become my guardian angel?

This was preposterous.

How could I explain the last few hours?

Suddenly frightened, I struggled to force my mind to go blank. I was getting a headache and wanted to get home, lie down on the couch, and force myself to relax. I only hoped I wouldn't have the same unwanted visitor.

Ten minutes later, I turned off Semoran and onto the narrow two-lane paved road that took me to my condo development.

"Miss me?" asked the irritating voice in the seat beside me.

Although I feared he'd eventually return, I still jerked in surprise and nearly lost control of the wheel.

"Watch it. You'll kill us both. Oh, wait!" He chuckled. "You *can't* kill me. I'm already dead!"

I bit my lip as I rounded the curve and eased the BMW down the straight stretch that took me to my building.

Then, just as I pulled into my drive, I discovered that dead silence had thankfully returned.

***

I knew better than assume that he'd gone so quickly, so it didn't surprise me to hear his voice in the hall entrance the moment I pushed open the front door.

"The master returns," he said, chuckling. "What can I get you, kind sir? Your pipe? Slippers? How 'bout a nice wine from the cellar? A pricey Bordeaux, perhaps?"

"Oh, shut up." I slammed the door and marched down the tiled foyer, totally ignoring his essence on my way to the kitchen.

"What's wrong, honey?" he quipped, chuckling. "Rough day at the office? Heavy rush hour traffic? Oh, wait! You left work early, didn't you?"

I tossed the keys onto the kitchen counter. "You know damned well I left early."

"Good gosh, what an attitude! What happened, honey? Someone piss in your coffee cup? Dump a load on your bagel? Throw up on your honey bun?"

"You know damned well what happened. And *don't call me honey!*"

"My, my... Where's this flare of temper coming from? Pressure at the office? Oh, wait! I think I know... It was that thing with the bald guy, wasn't it? What's his name? Frisbee? He embarrassed ya, didn't he? And in front of all your peers..."

"Shut up. You know damned well what's wrong. And the man's name is *Frisdale*."

I wanted a drink—a strong one—but since my hangover hadn't quite gone, I decided to settle for a cup of strong black coffee.

58

I rinsed out the pot and struggled to keep from losing my cool—or tossing the pot. As I grabbed a cup, I sensed that his essence had moved closer to the table.

"Get the hell away from my table." I knew he was dead, but it irritated me to imagine him so close to where I ate my dinner. I didn't want him here in the first place. I wanted him gone.

"Frankie-boy...I'm dead, ya know."

"Get away from my table."

"In other words, I'm not actually *here*—if ya know what I mean."

"I sincerely wish you weren't *anywhere* I am. Not even in the same county. Or *state!*"

"I was gonna say that I'm not really here, so my form won't actually disturb anything—"

"It's disturbing the hell out of *me!*"

"Frankie..."

"The name is *Frank*. And get the hell away from my table!"

Silence. A second later, his voice sounded like it had moved over to the kitchen window. "Better?"

"No."

"Where *would* ya like me to be?"

I shrugged. "Somewhere in downtown Detroit, maybe. Or how about Upstate New York? I hear Albany's nice this time of year."

"You're not making a fella feel very welcome, ya know..."

"Apparently I'm not making you feel *un*welcome, am I? Not enough for you to leave me in peace..."

59

"Tell me what's wrong. Maybe I can—"

"As I said before, you know damned well what's wrong. You know because you're the *cause* of what's wrong!"

"That hurt, Frankie."

"*Frank*. But it didn't hurt quite enough, did it?"

"Why do ya say that?"

"Because *you're still here*!"

"But Frankie... I'm your guardian angel. I *should* be here. It's my job."

"*Frank*. And that's one thing I don't understand."

"What's that?"

"What makes you think you're a guardian angel? And even if you *were* one of them, what would make you think you're *my* guardian angel?"

"That's *two* things, actually."

"Wow. You can actually *count*."

"You're chock-full of the hurties today, ain'tcha?"

"You've given me good reason for tossing a slew of them at you. Just answer my question—or, to be precise, *questions*."

"If I wasn't your guardian angel, why do I keep showing up where you are?"

"Because I was stupid enough to visit you at your grave, and you decided to stick to me like a seriously bad rash."

"A tad disgusting, maybe, but it does sound reasonable. And it does show that you cared enough about the ol' Bruceter to come see me at—"

60

"I went to the grave to see if the ol' Bruceter's name was etched into the marker. I wanted to see it to believe it."

"That's really touching, my man."

"I'm *so* glad you think so."

"But that still doesn't answer my question."

"Which one is that?"

"Why do you suppose I keep comin' here if I wasn't s'posed to?"

"I wish I knew. But if I *could* provide a helpful answer, I'd say that you really ought to try showing up somewhere else."

"Now why would I wanna do that?"

"You need to see if your next victim appreciates the experience even more than I do. Then maybe you should consider sticking around *them*, rather than bugging *me*."

"Now what would be the fun in that?"

"By the way, how the hell are you actually *helping* me? You pop up at the most inconvenient times and torment me until I lose my composure. Then I say something—usually in front of other people—which makes them think I'm ready for the rubber room. In other words, how are you *helping* me?"

"I guess I'm gonna have to work a tad more on my technique, then."

"Technique? Is *that* what this is?"

"What *what* is?"

"The pestering. The smartassed remarks. Showing up and embarrassing me in front of my co-workers."

"Hey, I'm new at this. I'm new at being dead, ya know. So cut me a little slack."

"I'd love to, but since you're already dead, a noose wouldn't work very well on that scrawny neck."

"Honestly, Frankie-boy, where's all this animosity coming from?"

"The name is *Frank*. Can you still see yourself in the mirror?"

"I suppose so. Why?"

"Go have a look, then."

"Now why would I wanna—" Just then, he chuckled. "I get it. Good one, Frankie! You can come up with some real zingers at times. That one was a first-class knee-slapper!"

The coffee was ready. I poured a cup, dropped some sugar into it, went over to the table, and sat down. As I sipped, I stared straight ahead and hoped he'd get the message that I didn't want to talk anymore.

"I'm not exactly getting a warm fuzzy from ya, Frankie..."

I didn't reply.

"Something tells me you'd like it if I left ya alone for a little while."

I couldn't believe he'd said that. "That's the first intelligent thing you've said since you bulled your way into my home."

"I really don't wanna leave right now, but I got this feeling time's run...out...again."

His voice, thank God, had already begun fading.

I felt relief for the first time since he'd appeared in my car. "Sounds to me that your voice has the right idea. Listen to it. Take its lead and go look for it. And when you do find it, *please* take it somewhere else."

"Damn... Just when things...getting interesting..."

"Don't let me stop you."

"I'll...back, Frankie. And when...do, I'll show ya...I really *do*..."

"Please don't hurry. And it's *Frank*, dammit!"

Once again, the sudden silence was wonderful.

***

For the next few minutes, I listened to the wonderful silence, expecting to hear his exasperating voice.

I heard nothing.

Despite my suspicions, I seemed to be alone.

My nerves still jittery, I carefully raised the coffee to my lips and had a refreshing sip, hoping that it would help get my nerves back under control. I needed a few minutes of peace and quiet and knew this would not happen unless Cavanaugh stayed away. Judging by how my luck had been lately, I expected him back at any moment, chuckling at my reaction.

Just then, the thought came to me, and I could feel the tension disappearing as if by magic.

What would happen if I didn't react at all? What would he do? Would he eventually get bored and vanish? What fun would it be for him,

63

performing to an audience of one who ignored him completely?

It reminded me of a girl I had a crush on in high school—a tall, slender brunette named Carol. An extremely popular cheerleader, she was my ideal woman at the time, and I did everything imaginable, short of setting my hair on fire, to get her to notice me. But despite my efforts, she didn't acknowledge the fact that I was alive. After months of anguish and self-hatred, I realized that she would never care about me, so I stopped trying altogether.

Would Cavanaugh stop trying if he failed to get a reaction?

I continued drinking my coffee while gathering the courage to do what I'd just decided.

After several minutes, he still hadn't reappeared.

I finished my coffee and waited.

Still nothing.

I got up, went to the counter, poured another cup, and went back to the table. And waited.

After ten minutes, he still hadn't returned.

I glanced at the wall clock. He'd been gone more than twenty minutes, possibly thirty. Was this how long it took him to recharge?

I wondered how much longer it would take. Five minutes? Ten? If so, what could I do in ten minutes?

Enjoy this second cup of coffee? Watch something on Netflix? Would I be ready for him when he reappeared? Would I still have my argument ready?

Did I really *want* to have another argument with him?

So far, my batting average with him had been miserably low. He barely listened to anything I said. Even when he did, he always came back with a pun, or some other remark that destroyed my train of thought.

What would he say if I told him that he kept coming back to me because he liked watching my reaction?

I already told him how I felt—what good had that done?

Telling him my thoughts would do no good at all. He would react by saying something funny or stupid about it—which would antagonize me all over again.

I wondered if I could elude him by getting in my car and making tracks. Was it possible? Or was I expecting something that wasn't in the charts?

What had been happening during the last twenty-four hours wasn't exactly in the charts, was it? A jerk from my childhood coming back from the dead to annoy me for the rest of my life?

What sort of textbook could explain something like *that*?

In any event, what did I have to lose?

I put down my cup, crossed the room, grabbed my keys, and rushed outside. Then I jumped in my car, flicked on the ignition, and backed out of the drive.

A couple of minutes later, I pulled onto Semoran Boulevard and headed south.

***

Despite the heavy southbound flow, I reached Fashion Square Mall in just fifteen minutes.

I sensed that I was still alone as I pulled into the side lot of the huge shopping complex and parked about twenty spaces down from the main entrance.

It was close to dinnertime. The lot was already nearly packed. It was painfully obvious that Cavanaugh could sniff out my vibes, but a heavy crowd might possibly make it more difficult for him. He probably wouldn't like it at all when he returned to the condo and didn't find me there.

The only thing that mattered was that it had been nearly forty minutes since I'd seen him. A ponderous weight had been lifted from my shoulders. I felt invigorated, and for the first time since I'd woken that morning, I discovered that I was famished.

The very thought of dinner made my mouth water.

I got out of the car and, whistling, walked briskly up the aisle, toward the building.

I entered the buffet restaurant feeling happy and carefree. The place was crowded. I joined the long line and, feeling somewhat safe, savored each moment of being by myself. I grabbed a tray and went down the aisle, picking up small dishes of brown rice, butter beans, sautéed mushrooms, a slice of apple pie, and a generous cut of charbroiled T-bone.

Once I paid the cashier, I sat down at a corner table, arranged my plates on the table, and handed my tray to the smiling hostess.

I was ready to relax and enjoy my meal when I suddenly heard the cursed voice dangerously close to my left ear.

"Miss me, Frankie-boy?"

My gut growled. "Like a giant carbuncle on my ass," I whispered between clenched teeth.

"Ouch. Still with the insults, eh?"

"I don't see any reason why I should stop now. Do you?"

"You really get testy when you've got something goin' on in your shorts, don'tcha?"

I had a sip of iced tea, picked up my knife, and sliced a juicy sliver of my steak. This meal looked and smelled heavenly. I intended to eat every bit of it and promised myself to do it even with Cavanaugh there, clinging to me like snot. It was going to be impossible to ignore him, but I was determined to try. I owed it to myself. "I'll be able to see things much clearer when you get the hell out of here and leave me alone." It was difficult to keep my voice down, but I managed.

I heard Cavanaugh sigh. "Well, god*damn*... You're really wound up pretty tight right now."

The steak was fabulous. Cooked over the open flame just the way I liked it. I enjoyed another sliver and a forkful of the sautéed mushrooms. The meal would be perfect if I could just focus on it.

For this, I would probably have to shift his attention to something else...

"There's a nice-looking redhead over there." I used my knife to point to the table about five down on my right, where an attractive woman in her early thirties had just sat down with two men in dark suits. "Go try out your charms on her. Maybe she'll appreciate it."

"How many times must I tell ya, Frankie-boy? I'm your guardian angel. I *can't* go to someone else. What would be the point?"

I had some rice and another slice of steak. I was beginning to feel much better. To my relief, this jerk wasn't bothering me as much now.

The waitress came over with a pitcher of iced tea. She was about nineteen and didn't weigh much more than a hundred pounds. Her thick blond hair was pulled back and tied in a ponytail that hung down between her shoulder blades. She was very pretty. I had the sinking feeling Cavanaugh was about to piss me off again.

"More tea?" she asked.

"Please."

She bent and poured some into my glass.

"Nice tight little ass." Cavanaugh chuckled. "That's the shitty thing about being dead. Ya can't even cop a good feel." He went silent. I suspected he was probably studying her. "Not much in the tit department, but as they say, anything more than a mouthful is a waste."

I thanked her. She smiled, turned, and went over to another table.

I ate more steak.

Nothing more from Cavanaugh. It made me wonder if he had taken my advice and drifted over to a table where two large-breasted women were having a lively chat as they ate their meal. Both wore short skirts. I could well imagine him dropping down and disappearing underneath the table.

About five minutes later, I'd nearly finished my steak and was savoring the rest of the sautéed mushrooms.

"Why do so many babes wear underwear nowadays?" His voice suggested that he had planted himself on the table facing me.

I wanted to tell him to get his ass off the table but knew that would start another argument. I didn't want to create a scene that might get me thrown out of the place. I just ignored him and concentrated on my meal.

"It just seems so unnecessary, doesn't it?" he asked. "Underwear? Panties? Really? They end up coming off anyway, right?"

I hoped my silence and lack of attention would eventually get to him. If I was lucky, he'd get bored and leave.

"You're not much of a chatterer right now, are ya, Frankie-boy?"

The apple pie was delicious. I made short work of it. Once I'd finished, I got up and went over to the coffee station to pour a cup of strong black coffee.

"What can I do to get you to realize I'm your boy, Frankie?" he said as I took my cup back to my table. "How can I convince you I'm your guardian? Your protector?"

I sipped my coffee and said nothing.

"What can I do? I mean really?"

The blonde came back and asked if I wanted anything else.

I imagined Cavanaugh moving closer in a feeble attempt to fondle her.

"I'm fine, thanks."

Smiling, she said, "Please come back and see us." She turned and hurried away.

"Yep, a real shame." Cavanaugh had obviously returned. "That babe's wearing panties, too. I checked. They're sheer, but they still manage to hide the good stuff. There really oughta be a fuckin' law about babes wearing underwear in public."

I didn't reply.

"By the way, while I was checking her out, I spotted this nice little brown mole on her left hip. It's right in the center of the hipbone. Ya can't miss it if ya pull down that skirt and enjoy a healthy gander before samplin' that primo stuff…"

Without replying, I got out my money and laid a ten-spot for her on the table.

"That's a pretty hefty tip, Frankie-boy…"

"She deserves it. And the name's *Frank*."

"You're a regular Boy Scout, ain'tcha?"

I finished my coffee, then got up and left.

***

I got behind the wheel of the BMW and immediately sensed his presence.

Sighing tiredly, I slipped the key in the ignition. "You just won't get it, will you?"

"What exactly don't I get, Frankie-boy?"

I turned on the ignition. "I don't want to *see* you anymore. I don't want you seeing *me*. I don't want to see—or hear—or smell—*any* sign of you. Anywhere. Ever again. And my *name*, goddammit, is *Frank*!"

"Smell, too? Wow. That's *really* cold. You sure don't take any prisoners when you're on the rag, do ya?"

I put the car in gear and eased out of the spot. "You asked."

"How can I make things right with ya, Frankie-boy—uh, Frank?"

I couldn't believe he'd asked such a ridiculous question.

"You're not serious."

"Don't I look serious?"

"How can I possibly tell *how* you look if I can't *see* you?"

"How do I sound?"

"Sarcastic. As always. Arrogant. Rude. Ignorant. Mean."

"Ouch."

"In other words, anything *but* serious."

"I'm serious. Believe me. Serious as a fuckin' heart attack."

He sounded serious, but I knew I couldn't trust him. "About what?"

"About makin' things right."

"You really want to know?"

"By all means. Just tell me."

"It's very simple. Just disappear, and never come back."

He was silent for about a minute. Then, just as I was getting quite comfortable during the lull, he disturbed me once again. "How about if I can prove to you that I'm really s'posed to be your guardian angel?"

I pulled out onto Semoran and joined the heavy northbound flow. "And just how the hell do you intend to do that?"

"I'll find a way."

"Then do it."

"Okay."

"When?"

"Soon."

"Really?"

"Yep."

"Okay. And while you're at it, do me a very large favor."

"And what would that be?"

"Disappear. And don't come back until you've found a way of convincing me that the heavens and the spirits in the universe have all joined together and decided to turn the remainder of my life on earth into a living hell by making it your job to look out for me."

"Wow... I'm seriously and totally wounded!"

"You asked and I told you, so do something about it."

He went silent again. Then, as I slowed down at the first four-way intersection, he said, "I can do that, Frankie—"

"*Frank*, dammit. And don't start calling me Frank Dammit!"

"I can do that, too."

"Great. 'Bye."

"Want me to leave right now?"

"Yes."

"Really?"

"Yes."

"Seriously?"

"Dammit, I want you to leave *right now*."

A heavy sigh. "Okay..."

I waited for him to disappear.

The light changed. As I joined the flow, I said, "You haven't disappeared, you know. I can tell. You know how I know? I have this sinking feeling in my gut. This tells me you're still right here."

"There's a good reason for that."

"I know this is going to be anything *but* good, but since you're gonna tell me about it no matter what, just go right ahead and spit it out."

"One thing we need to get settled before I disappear."

"What's that?"

"While I'm workin' on a way to prove myself, you gotta do a large favor for me in return."

I knew I was going to regret this, but I had to know what I was up against. "And what's that?"

"If I come back and give ya genuine proof that I'm your guardian angel, you gotta accept it."

"I will."

"All right, then. Say it."

"Say what?"

"Tell me you'll accept me as your guardian angel."

"I'll do that only if you can actually *prove* you're my guardian angel."

He thought that over.

After about a minute of silence, I said, "Okay?"

"Okay."

"Go away, then. Go wherever you have to go to find me proof."

Silence.

I stopped at the next red light and waited to hear another one of his stupid zingers.

I heard nothing but silence.

"Cavanaugh?"

Nothing.

"You still here?"

More silence.

I didn't say anything for another minute or so. I didn't trust him, so I gave him another minute. "Are you in the back seat?"

No reply.

"You're actually gone? As in truly and absolutely gone?"

More silence.

The light changed. I eased forward.

About a mile later, after more blessed silence, I had the feeling that I was truly alone.

However, I knew better than lower my guard.

Cavanaugh had disappeared, but I strongly suspected I would be seeing him again…

Long before I was ready to.

***

Once I got back to the condo and discovered that I was still alone, I began to feel terrific.

For the first time that day, I experienced no stress or nausea. I wanted to laugh and maybe even perform a cartwheel. However, since I was still fighting that cursed hangover, I decided to take a few deep breaths and forget about doing anything that might possibly make me throw up.

I fixed some coffee, flicked on the TV, and watched a movie. After all that had happened that day, I finally felt myself relaxing. The coffee helped. Although I couldn't properly concentrate on the movie, I discovered that it didn't matter. I suddenly believed that things might turn out okay. And that made life worthwhile again.

I sincerely hoped Cavanaugh would stay away. I didn't want to count on the fact that I might never see him again—I knew better than rely on such foolish optimism—but I honestly felt that it might take him forever to figure things out. I had no idea what he would have to do to find his answer. As with most everyone, I was totally clueless about the Afterlife. I could only hope that the process would take weeks, perhaps months, before he would visit me again.

The optimist in me sincerely hoped that he might not reappear if he couldn't find proof that he wasn't my guardian angel, or even an angel at all.

Maybe he'd finally understand that he'd be much better off if he stopped tormenting me and left me forever in peace.

That was what bugged me most about all this. It wasn't the fact that I didn't actually *believe* in guardian angels… The reality was that I'd never been certain of *what* I believed. But even if I *did* believe, logic told me that if there was indeed an angel looking after me, he wouldn't appear at all, let alone torment me. And even if my angel *did* appear, I didn't think he would tell me who or what he was. And since Cavanaugh had been guilty of all three of these things, I just knew he wasn't what he claimed to be.

But what if I was wrong? What if he *was* what he'd claimed?

What if—

"No." I didn't even want to consider going down that path again.

I didn't want to admit to myself that I had done anything to deserve such a horrible fate.

***

Later that night, after watching a couple of TV shows, I decided to head off to bed.

I plodded into my bedroom, undressed, and slipped into bed. The small glass of red wine I'd had an hour earlier to help me relax was doing its job.

I was both grateful and relieved for being able to enjoy the evening alone. After just a few minutes, I began to drift off. I surrendered happily to the darkness falling softly over me, and before I knew it, I was asleep.

But not for long.

"Frankie? You asleep?"

The strange voice startled me. I sat up sharply. "What the *hell*?"

"You up?"

"I am now!" I strained to penetrate the darkness. "Who the hell is there?"

"It's me—who else?"

"Dammit!" I groped for the bedside lamp, nearly knocking it over as I clumsily flicked it on.

Although I couldn't see him, I could sense that he was hovering at the foot of the bed, watching me, and that he was probably giving me a stupid grin that would send me over the edge if I'd been able to see it.

"What the hell do you want? What the hell *is* this?" I glanced at my digital clock. Its luminous face said 3:19. "It's the *middle of the fucking night!*"

"I'm back, Frankie."

"Why the hell are you here?"

"I found out quite a few nifty things."

"And you couldn't wait until morning to tell me about them?"

"Time's different on this side, my main man. Everything's, well, it all meshes together, and we don't need clocks—"

"They sure as hell come in handy here!"

"That doesn't matter right now. The stuff I found out is really important."

I didn't like his tone. He sounded way too triumphant and happy for my taste. "I was *sleeping*, dammit!"

"I know. I could tell. You were snorin'. Did you know you snore, Frankie?"

"What the hell does *that* have to do with anything?"

"You don't have adenoids, do ya, my man?"

"Dammit, stick to the subject." I wanted this over with. His very presence was raking on my nerves. "Get on with it so you can get the hell out of here and *let me sleep!*"

"I'll get to it, Frank, but I don't think you'll wanna sleep when I'm finished."

"What the hell are you talking about now?" I asked fearfully.

"Just this, Frank. Ya won't like this much, but, well, the thing is, in a nutshell—"

"Get *to* it!"

"All right, then... To be blunt, I found out that I'm your boy after all."

"Boy?"

"Angel—what else?"

"You *can't* be serious."

"I know how that must sound to ya—"

"You can't possibly."

"Listen, Frank. When they told me what was going on—"

"*Who* told you?"

"Whazzat?"

"*Who* told you what's going on?"

"Frank, there's a bunch of activity goin' on over there."

"Where's *there*?"

"The other side—"

"I just want to know who told you."

"I don't know his actual *name* or anything—"

"Then how the hell do I know you're telling me the truth?"

"You're just gonna have to take my word for it."

"You can't be serious."

"Don't I *look* serious, Frank?"

"You've asked me that before. I can't see you. And believe me, I really, really like it that way."

"Listen, Frankie—"

"*Frank*. No. *You* listen. You're *not* my guardian angel. I refuse to believe something so depressing. And unless someone else from that other side of yours comes forward and tells me otherwise, I don't want to see you again. Or hear you. Is that clear?"

"Frank—"

"I *said*, is that *clear*?"

"Who would you believe if I brought 'em here?"

"Anyone but you…"

"That's cold, Frank."

"It's how I feel!"

"Listen. Say I can't find anyone to tell ya what's going on… How else can I convince you I'm on the up and up?"

"That's just it. You can't."

"But what if I'm right? What if I really *am* your guy? What if I'm what I say I am, and you botched it just 'cause you don't like some of the things I've been doin'?"

"First of all, you're *not* my *guy*. Secondly, it doesn't *matter* what you say because I don't *believe* you. And thirdly, I didn't like *any* of the things you've been doing!"

"But Frank…I told ya why I was doin' all that shit. Everything was new and exciting. I was feelin' my oats. How would *you* feel if you just found out you were dead and could do some neat shit you couldn't do at all when you were alive? I just couldn't help myself."

"I don't care. Not one bit. I want you to leave and never come back. I want to be left alone."

"Frank—"

"You heard me."

"Would a sign convince ya I'm right about this?"

I thought about that for a moment. I knew he was up to something, but if this meant tripping him up again, I figured I should at least try it. What did I have to lose? "What *sort* of sign?"

"Anything that would tell you I'm right."

I wanted him gone. He was wearing me down, but I had to force myself to stay strong. I couldn't give in. But despite my efforts, I quickly found myself succumbing to exhaustion, and in my moment of weakness, I began thinking of a way out of this.

He mentioned a "sign." I considered it and realized that, despite my initial resistance, his idea might just work in my favor. What sort of "sign" could he possibly provide as positive proof? And unless he could actually bring some other spirit back with him to justify his ridiculous claim, I was confident he'd be totally out of bullets.

This might be all I needed to be rid of him once and for all.

"All right," I said finally. "You've got it. A sign might convince me otherwise."

I heard him sigh.

"It has to be legit, though. The sun coming up tomorrow morning just won't cut it. Neither will the hot water coming out of the H tap, or the toothpaste coming out of the tube without running all over my hand. It has to be something that wouldn't happen normally."

"Normally?"

"That's something you probably don't know too much about."

"Sometimes you really know how to hurt a guy, Frank."

"Good. But since you're not an actual *guy* anymore, that really doesn't matter to me. What matters is that you've got to produce a sign, or I'll never acknowledge you again."

"*Then* you'll believe me?"

"Maybe."

"Okay, then. I'll get ya your sign."

"And don't come back until you do."

Silence.

"Are you still there?"

More silence.

I flicked off the light, lay back down, and ignored my racing pulse as I tried to relax.

Sleep wouldn't come so easily this time.

I closed my eyes and tried once again to empty my thoughts of Cavanaugh and our latest conversation. It turned out to be much more difficult than I imagined.

Nonetheless, exhaustion finally won out, and in no time at all, I drifted off again.

CHAPTER 4 - THE THIRD DAY

After just a few hours of intermittent sleep, I awoke at eight o'clock.

Before getting out of bed, I spent the next few minutes waiting to hear any evidence of Cavanaugh's irritating presence. The wonderful silence made me realize I was alone once again.

Then I remembered our conversation just hours earlier.

Cavanaugh had agreed to show me a "sign" that he was telling me the truth—that he was my guardian angel. I told him his evidence had to be genuine. Until then, he couldn't reappear.

I hoped with all my heart that he would never find that sign. Until then, I could enjoy my newfound peace and quiet.

I got out of bed, lumbered to the bathroom, slipped into the shower, and stood under the warm spray. As the thick, powerful blast invigorated me, I tried convincing myself that everything would be all right. Cavanaugh would never reappear, and I could finally have my life back.

Ever vigilant, the eternal optimist in me refused to believe the worst.

Revitalized and hungry, I toweled dry, dressed, and padded down the carpeted hall to make breakfast.

The kitchen clock said 9:15.

I was in the process of making coffee when I decided to get my mail.

It was just another warm summer morning. Bright sun and a soft, light-blue sky peppered with tiny wisps of clouds floating around lazily like discarded pieces of string. The mail usually came early in my development, even on Saturdays, so I figured it had already been delivered.

I decided to take in some early morning fresh air to get the lungs working. I marched down the long, winding walk, turned the corner, and headed to the end of the block, where the silver tower of mailboxes servicing my complex sat on a thick metal post.

I used my key to open my box and pulled out the envelopes. There were several of them, mostly bills and advertisements, and as I pulled them out and closed and relocked my door, two pieces of mail dropped from my grasp and skipped from the pavement, onto the freshly mowed grass, before landing on the ground.

Frowning, I stepped off the sidewalk onto the grass. Just as I bent to pick them up, a distant roar reverberated down the avenue.

Something loud snarled and growled as it whizzed by me, missing me by inches.

A dark figure on a motorcycle slammed into the mail tower, sending it soaring into the air in a twist of jagged metal scraps. As the shards hurled toward the bushes, yards, and parked vehicles, the cycle toppled over and flipped several times, tossing its young male driver before slamming onto the pavement and sliding down the street, sending sparks dancing wildly and then ramming into a

84

parked SUV. It lay there, its rear wheel spinning wildly.

A second later, the driver landed with a loud thud directly across the street, sliding toward the curb in an irritating hush of leather.

I just stood there, watching stupidly as if viewing a scene from a TV show.

Once reality finally returned, my senses caused my mind to start functioning again. Then it dawned on me.

If the envelopes hadn't dropped onto the grass…

If I hadn't moved away from the tower just then…

Oh no…

Something else struck me just then.

Something horribly frightening and depressing.

This was the "sign."

Cavanaugh's proof that he was my guardian angel…

* * *

Half an hour later, after I made my statement to the cops and talked to the paramedics, a couple of my neighbors, and three very concerned senior members of our Housing Association, I trudged back up the walk and went back inside.

I soon found that my thought processes had ceased to function. I stood in the foyer, staring at my surroundings as if I had never even been here before. I quickly discovered that I could not concentrate on anything at all. As the images of the accident spun around wildly in my head, I went

85

over to the couch, collapsed into it, and stared numbly at the white drapes in the front window.

My mind had simply switched off. All I could see was the mail tower flying in the air like a flock of disoriented silver birds, the spinning tire of the motorcycle, and the biker lying near the bushes three doors down from the corner.

And, of course, the loud cackling of Bruce Cavanaugh in my head, followed by his telling me what he'd done to save my life, which proved he was my guardian angel.

I'd asked for a sign, hadn't I? I wanted some indication that would convince me that what he'd been telling me was the truth. I needed definite proof that would assure me that he hadn't been feeding me utter nonsense. A sign that he was truly my very own guardian angel.

At the time, I was confident that he wouldn't be able to provide any. I didn't like him, his behavior, his attitude, or anything that oozed out of his mouth. His actions alone convinced me that he had no right to be *anyone's* guardian angel.

But because of what had just happened, I had to accept the fact that Cavanaugh had been chosen to watch over me for the rest of my life. Of all the people who had died during my lifetime, all the people I had ever known, I ended up with Cavanaugh.

I sat stiffly on the couch and wondered what had gone wrong with my life. Something certainly had. Otherwise, why would I end up with a guardian angel I didn't even want—someone I didn't respect or even care for? He had just saved my life, but I didn't care. I didn't want him near me, so what good had it done for him to save my life? I would have preferred taking a direct hit from that motorcycle. I would rather have been given the choice of being hauled to the emergency room with life-threatening injuries than sit here in this distressed state, knowing what happened and realizing that Cavanaugh would return very shortly, gloating about what he'd just done.

"I'm doomed." That last word trickled out of my mouth softly, like the final groan of a dying man. And after what had just happened, I considered myself a dying man. Doomed. The term fit perfectly.

Although Cavanaugh had saved my life, all that mattered was that I was condemned to spend the rest of my days paying for it.

The situation made me want to scream.

I took a deep breath to get a good one going. But at the last moment, I gave up and let it shrink into a depressing groan.

Then, not knowing what else to do, I got up and went into the kitchen to make more coffee.

It wasn't until I reached for the refrigerator door that I realized I was still gripping my mail tightly in my left hand.

***

Once I began feeling slightly better, I decided to fix a sandwich.

I didn't want a full breakfast but figured I should eat something while I was still alone and thinking somewhat clearly. I didn't know what frame of mind I'd be in when Cavanaugh reappeared. I decided it would be to my advantage to have something in my stomach when the inevitable happened.

Anyway, I knew I should stop agonizing about what had happened earlier and try to get on with my day. No matter what I was doing, I knew damned well that Cavanaugh would eventually show up. When this happened, things would go down the tubes very quickly. Until then, I didn't want to think about him or what I would learn as the result of my near-death experience with the runaway motorcycle.

Just as I finished making my sandwich, I turned to put the mayo and mustard back into the fridge. This was when I sensed his irritating presence in the room.

"How long have you been here?"

"Just long enough to watch ya fixin' your sandwich. Ya know ya use too much mustard, don'tcha?"

I opened the refrigerator door and struggled to maintain an air of calm.

"You oughta stick to just a squirt or two. Anything more is wasted—know what I mean?"

I didn't want to get into any sort of mindless discussion that would prolong this. "Just get on with this so you can leave."

He shrugged. "I figured I oughta pay ya a visit. I'll bet ya know why, right?"

I put the mayo and the mustard on the shelf on the door. Then I grabbed a beer. I knew it was going to take my best effort to eat, but I should at least try. Once I finished talking with this idiot, I might not ever want to eat again.

I brought my beer, the sandwich, and a paper towel over to the table. "You came to gloat."

"Naw, just to tell ya how things work now."

I sat and had a swig of beer. "And just how do things work?"

I could tell he was watching me closely as I raised the bottle. Even though I couldn't see his form, I could imagine him licking his lips.

Once I'd lowered the bottle, he said, "What I wouldn't give to have one of those again..."

Seeing this golden opportunity, I wasted no time. "You can't. You're dead. You can't drink anything ever again." I genuinely enjoyed saying that. I'd never been one for harassing people, but Cavanaugh had a talent for bringing out a darkness inside me I never knew existed.

"Thanks for remindin' me."

"Don't mention it." I had another sip of beer—for his benefit. "So...how do things work?"

"You've heard the phrase, 'one hand washes the other?'"

I could tell exactly where this was going but decided to force him to proceed. "What does that have to do with anything?"

"I'm sure you can guess what I'm sayin'..."

I ate a little of my sandwich. "Maybe I'd like it spelled out for me. I'm sure you're just the man—or whatever the hell you are—to do it."

"Well, Frank, it's like this. I saved your life, right?" Before I could comment, he added, "I mean, there ya were, all set to get your mail, when this dickhead on a cycle loses control and damn-near turns ya into someone's sloppy hood ornament." He sighed heavily. "A second later? You might be sittin' here with me, just as dead as I am."

I put the rest of the sandwich back on the plate and gawked at it. He'd just spelled it out for me. He was right. If I hadn't moved off the walk to pick up those envelopes...

"Nothin' to say?"

I still had no idea if he'd saved my life. I knew all about fate and circumstance. I also knew how little it took to change destiny, how something trivial could alter the future. I immediately shifted my thoughts back to my visiting his grave. But instead of cursing myself once again for that colossal blunder, I forced my attention back to my present dilemma.

Had Cavanaugh saved my life? Or was there more to this I hadn't actually considered?

Had he somehow been instrumental in its outcome? Had he *influenced* it in some bizarre way?

I realized the moment I'd asked myself those two questions that finding out what happened would not be easy. Cavanaugh would not be truthful with me, especially with something like this. And he certainly wouldn't tell me the truth if it didn't put him in a bargaining position.

But it didn't matter. I had to try.

"Just one thing," I said finally. "How the hell did you work that?"

"The tricky little dodge-ball thingy with the cycle?"

"That's what we're talking about, isn't it?"

"Simple, my main man. I just made the envelopes drop from your hand."

"Why?"

"I saw the motorcycle coming at you."

"He could've just zipped right on past."

"But he didn't, did he?"

"How'd you know?"

"I just did."

"Let me guess. You're clairvoyant."

"Let's just say I can sense things much easier on this side. When you're a spirit, you get to see the clearer picture. Kinda like a panoramic view."

"And you actually *sensed* that bike was going to run me down?"

"I was right, wasn't I?"

There was something about the whole thing that didn't *feel* right. Something about it felt very *wrong*. I didn't know if I could prove it, I only knew how I felt. But since I knew I wasn't going to get any farther with this right now, I had to put this conversation to rest. "I guess so."

"Good. We're finally on the same page."

"And what page is that?"

"The page that says, 'one hand washes the other.'"

His tone sounded both logical and ominous. I was getting a bad feeling about this. I had another swig of beer and waited. I knew it wouldn't take him long to tell me what was on his mind.

"Curious?" he asked.

"I figure you'll tell me what you want. I also figure I'm not going to like whatever you've got in mind, so I'm really in no rush to hear it."

He laughed. "That's what I like about ya, buddy-boy. Ya say what's on your mind."

"I'm *so* glad you approve."

"So here we are, chattin' away like old buds. I just saved your life. Now you're gonna show your gratitude by doin' somethin' for me. How's that sound?"

"As I just said, it sounds like something I'm not going to like. But you're gonna go on with this anyway, so..."

"Well, I did save your life, you know..."

"You've already mentioned that once or twice before."

"Anyway, I figure that since ya owe me, it wouldn't be too much if ya paid a visit to see my ex-girl Mona."

"Now why would I want to do something like that?"

"She's got somethin' of mine."

"What could she possibly have that would be of any value to you now?"

"Money."

This made even less sense than before. "Why would you even care about that? You're dead. Money means nothing to you anymore."

"It shouldn't, but it does."

"And why would that be?"

"She dumped me, Frank. I figure she owes me. Big-time."

"Even if she does, why the hell would you even care about her anymore?"

"I don't care about her, Frank, I care about that money."

"Why?"

"It was my money. I had a whole bunch of it saved. I was gonna spend it on her, but when she dumped me—"

"Now you want it back."

"Yeah."

"Why? As I just said, you don't need it anymore."

"I still want it."

"But why?"

"I have a mother. I even have a sister. My mom, well, she ain't doin' too well lately. Sis, she's got this waitress job in some crappy low-class diner on the Trail. Tips aren't too great in that place, and she busts her ass six days a week for ten, sometimes twelve hours a pop. This is ten grand we're talkin' about, and both of 'em could really use—"

"You'd rather they get your money than Mona?"

"Damn straight. Mona's one uppity bitch. She's one of those babes, all she's gotta do is look at a guy and she's got him, and those long, sharp nails are hell on your short curlies—know what I mean?"

"Why'd you stick with her if she's such a bitch?"

"Why else? She can pull chrome."

I just sighed.

"When she stares a guy down, she might as well have those talons grippin' the dude's 'nads like a vise. Anyway, my mom needs the money. So does Sis. Why the hell should Mona keep it when she dumped me?"

"She shouldn't."

"Get that money for me, take it to my mom's, and we'll be all square. Ya won't see me again till I do ya another favor. That's how it's s'posed to work."

No matter how he phrased it, this still felt very *wrong*.

"Problem?" he asked.

"Maybe..."

"Let's hear it."

I shrugged. "From all I've read and heard about, I just thought an angel stood by—invisible and unseen, of course—and quietly steered whoever he was assigned to away from danger."

"That's what I just did this morning, right?"

"Well, yes, but—"

"But what?"

No matter what he said, nothing I had ever read or learned as a child in Catechism Class suggested that anyone was supposed to return a favor as payment for a good deed their guardian angel did for them. "I didn't know I'd have to do anything in return."

"It seems only fair, don't it?"

"I'm not sure if something like this should—"

94

"Just do me this one favor, 'kay? Ya do it and it'll be a while before ya see me again. How's *that* sound?"

"It sounds really great. Fantastic. Beyond words. Brilliant. I've got goosebumps just thinking about it. I could probably even do a cartwheel—"

"Don't go overboard, now. It's settled, then."

"I see some problems, though."

"Like what?"

"I don't know where Mona lives."

"I'll take ya there."

"But how will I know what I'm supposed to do? Or where the money is? Or—"

"I'll be right there with ya. I'll make sure ya get there, and I'll be guidin' you all the way."

"She won't be able to see you, will she?"

He laughed. "I don't think anyone can see me, buddy-boy…"

"Thank God for small favors…"

"Why'd ya even ask me?"

"I just don't want any surprises."

"Good one." He chuckled.

I was getting tired of this. "So…when do we do this?"

"Tonight. It has to be between ten and two in the morning."

"Why's that?"

"Those are her hours."

"Where does she work?"

"She does a spot at Rochelle's, on the Trail."

"That's a strip club."

"You got it."

95

"Let me guess. Mona's a stripper."

Cavanaugh laughed. "You're a quick study, Frank."

***

Mona lived in an attractive yellow stucco three-bedroom Spanish villa on Oak Ridge Road.

Green shutters framed the windows. The house sat comfortably behind a neat row of well-trimmed bushes, flowers, and palmettos. The mowed grass gave the property a warm, inviting appearance.

Something just didn't feel right about all this. I personally didn't know any strippers, but I did know a little about single women working nights. A young woman working such odd hours at a tough, demanding job would sleep most of the day and would not care much about lawn maintenance.

I parked along the curb on the opposite side of the street. "How does she find the time to tend to that yard?"

Cavanaugh laughed. "Mona wouldn't know a pair of prunin' shears from a chainsaw. She pays somebody to keep up the place."

"I guess she makes quite a bit at the club."

"If Mona knows anything, it's how to take her clothes off."

"Is that where you met her?"

"Where else could a guy like me meet such hot babes?"

I saw no point in continuing the discussion. He was right, but that didn't concern me. I didn't want to be here in the first place and promised myself to finish this nasty business as quickly as possible.

It was 10:15. The neighborhood was quiet, and there was no traffic. I was confident I could accomplish what we'd set out to do in just a few minutes.

"How do I get in?"

"There's a spare key under the flowerpot next to the mat in the back. It opens the back door. Go around to the back and snatch the key. I'll letcha know what to do from there."

"But once I get in—"

"Uh-oh…" Cavanaugh's voice began fading. "Shit!"

"What's going on?"

"I'm l-losin'…juice!" His voice sounded far away, but I could clearly hear the terror in his words.

"Maybe we should hold off on this until you can—"

"God*dammit*!"

"I can't do this without—"

"Frankie…think we…"

His voice sounded far away and muffled.

I fought down the growing panic. "Maybe we shouldn't—"

"Sorry, dude…just do…what I…and get the…"

Then he was gone.

"Cavanaugh?"

Silence.

"Give me a sign, dammit. Anything will do."

Nothing.

I took three deep breaths. I could do this. I had to. Otherwise, I'd have to stay here until he

97

reappeared. If I didn't act on this right now, I would never get any peace from him again.

I got out of the car, crossed the dark street on feet I could barely feel, and made my way down the front walk. I crossed the front yard and circled around to the back, until I reached the rear stoop. The backyard was relatively large: palmettos, some lounge furniture, even a barbecue pit about twenty feet from the privacy fence running along the back.

I found the key beneath the flowerpot, walked up to the back door, and pulled open the screen.

The key worked; the door opened easily.

My heart pumped loudly as I slipped inside.

It didn't take long to discover that if Cavanaugh had been right, Mona also paid someone to do the housekeeping. The house was strategically lit, possibly to discourage anyone from thinking no one was home. Night lights brightened the hall. A table lamp bathed the living room in a warm golden hue. An overhead light enhanced the foyer, and a hood bulb above the stove cast a yellow haze in the kitchen.

The house could have been used as a model right out of *Better Homes & Gardens*. The kitchen practically gleamed; the sink and counter glowed like polished gems. Even the drainer appeared to be from a magazine—the silverware placed neatly in individual compartments, the dishes leaning in their slots. I saw no evidence of dust, soap streaking, spillage, or garbage. The floor even sparkled in the hazy lighting.

A stripper with OCD? Once again, I began wondering if Cavanaugh had told me the truth about this woman.

Suddenly curious, I scanned the room.

"You here…anywhere?" I whispered nervously.

No response.

"Are you back yet?"

Silence.

He obviously hadn't had enough time to fully recharge.

Gathering courage, I proceeded down the carpeted hall.

The master suite sat at the end of the hall on the left. Since both table lamps beamed on a low setting, I immediately saw that the bedroom was just as neat as the kitchen. There were no clothes or underwear lying on the bed, the floor, or draped over the cedar chest or chair. The bed looked like it had been fixed by a Marine—pulled tight, no wrinkled corners showing. The ceiling fan scattered cool air lazily over the area. As with the rest of the place, I saw no dust or any other sign of imperfection.

I went over to the end table on the right side of the bed, where Cavanaugh had apparently hidden his money in the bottom drawer. I pulled it out. Inside were several journals and a couple of Manila envelopes. I placed them on the carpet beside the drawer. Then I fished through the pile, looking for a thick white envelope containing hundred-dollar bills.

There was nothing.

I was just about to get angry when I heard the front door open and close loudly.

***

My heart pounded wildly.

Luckily, a voice somewhere in my head had not yet succumbed to the panic and slammed my brain with an urgent message: *Put everything back—NOW!*

I hurriedly replaced everything and quickly closed the drawer. Then, just as I got down on my hands and knees, I heard someone coming down the hall. The footsteps were quick. I dropped to my belly and began sliding underneath the bed.

However, I quickly discovered that I had run out of time.

Someone stopped at the doorway.

"Who the fuck's in here?" It was a woman's low-pitched raspy voice, and she sounded angry.

I tried one last time to disappear as silently as possible beneath the bed.

The clicking of a pistol echoed loudly in the room, and for a moment I thought my heart would hammer its way out of my chest.

"Come out right now or I'll shoot."

I hesitated.

"I'm a damned good shot, and I don't think I can miss at this range. This mag holds eight, by the way. That means I've got eight tries to nail your ass."

My God. An enraged female with a gun. Could things get any worse?

My heart continued thumping heavily. I was certain she could feel it vibrating the floor beneath her feet.

"One last chance, buster. The police'll be on my side and you fucking well know it…"

Shivering, I crawled back out from under the bed, pushed myself up, and knelt facing her. I raised my arms, but it was difficult. They weighed a ton.

I soon saw that she hadn't been lying to me. She had a gun in her hands. It was silver and looked enormous—although I was sure my imagination had made it ten times bigger than its actual size. However, its size wasn't what I was most concerned about. It was the angry black hole at the end of the barrel that made my bladder ready to vent. The damned thing looked big enough to accommodate something the size of my index finger. I wasn't very familiar with guns but could figure out that this one was a large caliber model, and these boys made a substantial hole no matter what they hit.

She gripped the weapon in both hands, holding it dead-steady. This frightened me even more. I suspected that she not only knew how to use it but had used it in the past. As my eyes moved nervously from the gun to her face, I realized that her appearance concerned me just as much as her gun.

This woman could not possibly be a stripper. She was too old, for one thing, and too heavy, for another. To make matters even more puzzling, she was no beauty. She had a broad, moderately attractive face, but the fact that she was clearly closer to fifty than forty convinced me Cavanaugh had lied about her. Apparently this woman was not Mona, but if she was, she was no stripper.

This lady was dressed tastefully—blouse, slacks, matching jacket, and open-toed black sandals with four-inch heels. Her thick black hair was professionally done—brushed straight back and tied with a gold barrette that let it fall freely, stopping at least three inches short of her broad shoulders.

"All right." Keeping the gun trained on me, she moved over to the chair in the corner and lowered herself. It was only then that I noticed the large designer handbag hanging by a thick leather strap from her left forearm. Once situated, she freed her hand from her grip and, holding the pistol in her right hand, let the bag drop gently to the carpet. She then returned her left hand to its former position of holding the butt of the gun. She spent the next minute or so sizing me up. I could feel my resolve crumbling and my nerves beginning to quiver, but I knew better than move.

She watched me closely, her cold green eyes taking me in from the top of my head, down to my knees. "Now you can tell me who the hell you are and what you're doing here."

"Are you going to keep that gun aimed at me?"

"Don't change the subject. Now...who the hell *are* you?"

"It's making me nervous."

"It's supposed to, you idiot. To repeat...who the fuck *are* you?"

"Can't you just put it in your lap? I promise I won't do anything. I'm too scared, actually—"

"Cut the bullshit. One last time. Who in heaven's name *are* you?"

It was plain that she wasn't going to lower the gun, so I figured I'd better do as she said.

"I'm Frank Langley." I saw no need to lie. If she shot me, she'd check my pockets and find my wallet. If she spotted a discrepancy, she'd probably finish me off if she hadn't already.

"All right, Frank Langley. What the hell are you doing in my bedroom?"

I was too frightened to say anything. I couldn't possibly tell her why I was here. She would think I was insane. And judging by what had been happening to me the last couple of days, I'd have to agree with her. But I had to come up with *some*thing, and fast.

Before I could respond, she said, "In case you think you're gonna squeak out of this, I'd better explain something to you. My business partner is on his way here directly. He should be here any time now. He's not someone you want to mess around with, either."

This situation was getting even worse. With my luck, her "business partner" was someone who enjoyed breaking fingers and smashing toes and kneecaps. I knew I shouldn't think the worst, but this woman wasn't helping matters. She was sitting ten feet away, holding a large-caliber gun dead-steady on me as if it were the most natural thing in the world. I'd have to be a moron to expect her partner to be the shrinking violet type.

"Do you understand the situation now?"

Swallowing loudly, I nodded.

"I'm glad we're on the same page. See, I'm not too wild about sitting here like this, holding a gun on some stupid jerk who just broke into my place. I've got a zillion things to do tonight—receipts to file, paychecks to cut. I'm also tired and damned hungry. I'd much rather be in the kitchen, fixing a snack before doing the books and heading off to bed. It's been a long day, and I'm tired." She pointed to her high heels. "It's a bitch, walking around in these all day."

For some reason, I was suddenly relieved. Maybe it was because she just gave me a subtle hint that she wasn't all that eager to shoot me.

I decided to take a gamble and rely on her sense of decency.

"You really don't have to keep sitting there, you know. You could get on with your bookkeeping. Or fix your snack, if you wish. I promise I won't bother you."

She sighed. "You know what? I'm even less thrilled about someone breaking into my place when he turns out to be a dumbass who thinks I'm a complete idiot. This tells me how much simpler things would be if I just shot your ass right now and let my business partner decide what to do with your corpse."

So much for her sense of decency...

"Then by all means, keep the gun trained on me."

"Thanks for the advice. I think I'll do just that. Anyway, blood's impossible to get out of carpeting, and I just had this one replaced." She shook her head. "The prices they charge for carpeting nowadays…"

I glanced at the floor. "It's very nice. Looks expensive…and very tasteful."

"Enough of the bullshit, Langley. One last time—what the hell are you doing here?"

I tried a long shot. "You're not Mona, are you?"

Her thin, painted black brows squeezed together. "Who?"

Cavanaugh, you asshole, if I ever get out of this…

But I knew I shouldn't be surprised. I was disgusted with myself for letting him get me involved in this.

"I was told by a friend that someone named Mona lived here—"

"Who's your friend?"

"His name is Bruce Cavanaugh."

She thought about that for a moment. "Never heard of him."

"I already got that."

"He obviously lied to you."

"I got that, too."

"Why'd you come here? What's all this breaking-in crap have to do with someone named Mona?"

105

My mind worked feverishly to turn this insane fiasco into some semblance of logic. "Cavanaugh told me his girl Mona's a stripper at Rochelle's. Apparently she—"

"Rochelle's?" She sat up.

"Ever heard of it?"

"I should. I own the place."

My heart skipped a beat. Cavanaugh had apparently told me part of the story, but not the part I really needed to know.

"Go on..."

"Well, if you own Rochelle's, you must know Mona."

"I sure would—*if* someone named Mona worked there."

I sighed tiredly. "Let me take a wild guess. No Mona works at Rochelle's?"

"You got it, ace."

Cavanaugh, I'm gonna get you for this...

"Get on with your story."

"Anyway, he told me Mona has his money lying in a drawer beside her bed. He wanted me to get it for him."

"And he gave you this address?"

"I wouldn't be here, otherwise."

"How'd you get in? I didn't see any signs of forced entry, but I really didn't have a chance to check." She glared. "If you broke *anything*—"

"He told me about the key under the flowerpot near the back door."

She narrowed her eyes. "This Cavanaugh bastard...he *knew* about the key?"

"As I just said, I wouldn't be here unless—"

"And why couldn't this asshole friend of yours handle his little errand himself?"

I knew right then that I had to start being vague. If I told her the truth, it would end very badly. I also still had that feeling that she really didn't want to shoot me but would not hesitate if she felt threatened, or thought she was in the presence of a crazy person. "He's kind of...incapacitated right now."

"You're saying this asshole is in the hospital?"

"You could say he's in really bad shape, yeah."

"And he wanted you to do his dirty work for him?"

I nodded.

"He must have something on you..."

"Well, he *is* a fairly good...uh, friend..." I nearly choked on that last word, but I had to sound convincing. "He's done a favor or two for me in the past. He promised to pay me back if I did this for him..."

"Why didn't he at least give you the right address?"

"That's something I really need to ask him...if, that is, I can get out of this alive..."

She thought about that for a few moments. "That all depends on what my partner wants to do when he gets here."

I tried a long shot. "If you want to call the police, I'll totally understand."

She stiffened at the word "police." "That won't...be necessary."

107

Her reaction told me that she wasn't exactly on good terms with the cops. Otherwise, she would have already called this in. I realized right then that this could work in my favor. "I probably would do the same thing if I were you. The cops are paid to do stuff like—"

"You're not me," she said.

I needed to know what was going on. I couldn't possibly outsmart her, and I couldn't move an inch without her shooting me. But I figured I should know what to expect from here on in. "What do you think your partner will do when he gets here?"

"As I said before, he's not someone to mess around with."

"Bad-tempered, eh?"

"He doesn't like complications. We run a popular club and have learned a few things over the years. Complications cause even more complications. Russ likes things simple."

"Russ?"

"He's been running clubs here for years, and he's good at it. The two of us have been doing a terrific and profitable job running this one."

"I've heard a lot of good things about Rochelle's."

"Cut the crap. By the way, what did you find in those drawers?"

"Nothing. I was just looking for my friend's money. I didn't care about anything else."

Her forehead wrinkled. "What money?"

"He said he had ten thousand dollars in hundreds in a white envelope—"

Just then, the front door slammed shut.

The woman smiled, but it wasn't a pleasant one. "I guess it's time you met Russ."

***

The approaching footsteps sounded light, but quick.

When they were about halfway down the hall, I heard a high-pitched voice. "Shelley?"

The woman didn't take her eyes off me. Nor did she lower her gun. "In here, babe. We've got company."

The footsteps stopped abruptly. "C-Company?" The voice sounded much closer.

"Yeah. The unwanted variety."

The steps resumed, the last few much quicker. A moment later, he was standing in the doorway, gawking at me as one might eyeball something disgusting.

My first instinct was to laugh. However, the situation—as well as the huge gun pointing at me—kept me from humiliating myself with a snicker and suffering a quick and painful death by swallowing a large bullet.

The man standing in the doorway looked about sixty. He was bald, with thick-framed glasses and small, blinking eyes. He was clean-shaven and, although we were at least twenty feet apart, I could clearly see that he was wearing heavy makeup.

However, his facial features weren't what made this situation amusing.

This man was not much taller than five-two or -three, and very slender, tipping the scales at maybe

109

a hundred and twenty pounds after a heavy meal. He was dressed immaculately, the cut of his suit suggesting he had money. The charcoal-gray jacket and slacks were possibly imported. So were the patent leather tan Oxfords covering his tiny feet. His shoes had two-inch heels, telling me that this man was no more than five feet tall in his bare feet.

He wore large glittering rings on several fingers of each hand. His wristwatch—visible due to the tailored cut of his French sleeves, both of which were adorned with sparkling gold cufflinks—was either a Rolex or one of those German jobs that went for eighty grand.

If this was Russ, I wasn't in as much trouble as I thought. The woman was no doubt far more formidable than the slight, exquisitely dressed dandy barely visible in in the doorway. I didn't see a wrinkle or a crease anywhere on him. I couldn't imagine him doing anything that would dare smudge or pull the material of his expensive wardrobe.

"Who's *he*?" he asked, staring uncomfortably at me.

"Says his name's Langley. I caught him trying to slide underneath the bed."

"What's going on?" He was looking at me, but I could tell he wanted the woman to answer his question.

She jumped right in. "He says he came here to get money from a stripper named Mona, who works at Rochelle's. Says his friend Bruce Cavanaugh asked him to do it."

110

The man squinted behind his glasses. "Sir, I don't believe we have a...*Mona*...working for us..." The woman's name sounded like a grunt when he'd said it.

"I know. This lady gave me the good news a few minutes ago."

"I don't believe I have ever heard of a Bruce Cavanaugh, either..."

"I'm really not surprised."

He stared curiously at me. After nearly a minute, he said, "Are you armed, sir?"

"Of course not."

He turned to the woman.

"I didn't check." She stood. "I guess now's as good a time as any."

He stiffened. "I honestly don't want you doing that. I'd feel much better if you didn't get too close. He doesn't look dangerous, but nowadays, you can never tell..."

The woman continued watching me closely. "You're right, babe. He doesn't look very dangerous. Still, we need to find out for sure..."

"I think we'd better play it safe and have Ralph handle this for us. He's a pro."

Ralph? I felt my pulse hasten.

"You sure, babe? You know how he gets when—"

"I'll tell him to be gentle. You won't be a problem, will you, sir?"

"W-Who's Ralph?" I didn't feel as cocky as I did moments ago.

"Ralph is one of our bouncers. And, of course, my own personal bodyguard." Russ reached into his jacket pocket and removed a cell. "He's in the limo right now. He drives us everywhere. I'll have him come right in."

Suddenly terrified, I started to get up. I even pulled open my jacket. "I can show you right now that I'm not—"

"I wouldn't move if I were you." The woman had stiffened. Her gun twitched slightly but stayed trained on me.

"This shouldn't take long," Russ said. "Ralph is very good and extremely efficient with such procedures."

"I'm sure he is…" Even though I was kneeling, my knees were trembling so badly, I feared I'd lose my balance.

Cavanaugh, you bastard, if I ever get out of this alive…

"Ralph," Russ said softly into his cell, "would you come in here for a moment? I've got a small job for you…"

***

One minute later, a man the size of a forklift filled the doorway.

He was at least six-six, solidly built, and sported shoulders so wide that he had to turn slightly to get through the doorway. He was about thirty-five and good-looking in a dark, evil sort of way, with small, dark piercing eyes, a broken nose, and close-cropped black hair. Although he wore a dark, loose-fitting suit, his neck was visible above

112

his shirt collar. It was so thick and muscular that it made his head look small.

He stared at me for about three seconds before turning to the small man on his right, who barely came up to his chest. He said nothing, but I sensed a method of silent communication between boss and employee that only the two could clearly understand.

This made my situation even more frightening.

"Check him out, Ralph," Russ said. "See that he isn't armed. And please be gentle this time. Remember: this house belongs to Ms. Montclaire, and she hates cleaning up after a mess…"

My knees shook even worse.

Without a word, the monster crossed the room. It took him just two long strides to get to me. Before I had time to realize how close he was, he placed his enormous hands along my sides and, without any noticeable effort, pulled me into a standing position. He frisked me in just a few seconds, front and back, checking my jacket pockets, as well as my trousers, ankles, and the back of my shirt collar.

Anything?" his employer asked.

The monster didn't reply; I could only guess that he shook his head or sent his employer some sort of veiled expression.

A moment later, the woman pocketed her pistol and left the room.

Russ said, "Ralph, stand behind him and stay there until I say otherwise. I need to tell him something."

I knew better than turn around or do anything that might anger the beast. I could tell by how he handled me that I was nothing more than a fragile plaything he could have easily shattered into a million pieces. I weighed nearly a hundred and eighty pounds—which seemed to be no problem at all for his immense strength. But since he hadn't hurt me—at least not yet—I knew better than stretch my luck.

"Sir," Russ said, "I'm not quite sure that I believe your story. I've never heard of your friend Cavanaugh or this Mona person, and it troubles me greatly that you were able to get into the lady's home so easily. I do not like trouble, but sometimes it is unavoidable. However, I cannot have you coming back here and upsetting her again. In case you haven't figured this out by now, I am not someone who enjoys involving the police in private matters. In simple terms, I prefer handling my own affairs. Ralph is going to drive you away from this residence, and I never want to see you again. Do you understand?"

"You won't see me again, I promise."

"You don't have to promise, sir. Ralph will make sure of that."

Before I could let the grisly message sink in, the little man raised his eyes to the enormous figure standing behind me. "Ralph, make sure this gentleman relaxes comfortably during his ride."

A sudden blackness followed a sharp pain to the back of my neck.

Everything turned soft and fuzzy.

I woke up in the black, musty-smelling trunk of a moving vehicle.

The back of my neck throbbed. It felt as if it had been set on fire. I reached up and pressed my palm against the solid metal lid just a foot or so above me. I was about to panic when I heard a familiar voice next to my ear.

"Frank? You comin' to?"

It was Cavanaugh.

The moment I heard his voice, my hackles shot up in a bright hot flash. "You son of a bitch! What the hell *is* all this? What in heaven's name did you get me *involved* in?"

"I'll explain later."

"*Later*? Are you *insane*? I'm being taken somewhere out in the middle of nowhere to be dumped. I'm soon gonna be worm food, and you know what? Once I'm dead, I'm—"

"Frank, settle down. Relax."

"Settle *down*? *Relax*? You *can't* be serious!"

"I can getcha outa this."

"You'd *better*, dammit! You got me into it. Getting me out of it is the *least* you can do."

"Trust me, I'll—"

"*Trust* you?" I couldn't believe this jerk. "Are you out of your fucking *mind*?"

"Listen, Frank. Granted, that prob'ly doesn't sound like somethin' ya might wanna consider right now—"

"Ya think?"

"No matter how ya feel about me right now, I promise I'm gonna getcha outa this."

"Why'd you get me *into* this in the first place?"

"Later, Frank. I've got other things on my mind right now."

"You'd better tell me what this is all about, dammit!"

"Just as soon as I getcha outa here."

The vehicle began slowing down.

My pulse hastened. "You'd better think of something quick. There's a ginormous tank driving this car. He can pick me up with one hand and toss me around without breaking a sweat. I'm about to be dumped, and this is all because of something I was doing because, like an idiot, I believed what you told me."

No reply.

"Cavanaugh?"

Silence.

The big car slowed, pulled over, and stopped.

Panic scurried out of the shadows, smothering me. "Dammit, Cavanaugh!"

Footsteps.

A click.

The trunk lid raised open.

A huge, dark figure stood next to the bumper, looking down at me. The darkness of the night was so thick, I couldn't see his features. But it wasn't necessary. This was the same mastodon that had frisked me back in the woman's house on Oak Ridge, knocked me out, and tossed me in the trunk.

116

I could see a glint where his right hand should have been. He was obviously holding a gun.

"Out."

The glint twitched in his hand.

I'd run out of time.

"I ain't gonna say it again."

Cavanaugh, if you're gonna do something...

I was tempted to feign unconsciousness. I knew he wouldn't shoot me in the trunk. He'd have quite a mess to clean up. Judging by my brief encounter with Russ and Shelley, I figured they wouldn't accept any excuse for having the trunk of their limo spattered in blood. Ralph probably planned to haul me out of the trunk, lead me into the brush, shoot me, get back in the limo, and drive back to Oak Ridge Road.

Reluctantly I pushed myself up and carefully crawled out of the trunk. My neck hurt like hell, my head throbbed, and my joints were stiff from the cramped ride on the hard metal floor of the trunk. But I did as the monster ordered and slipped out of the confined space. Then, leaning against the bumper, I stared at the gigantic figure facing me just a few feet away and wondered how much time I had left.

"Start walkin'." The glint, now much closer, had transformed into a large silver pistol. He used it to motion to his right, which led to the woods.

Unable to think clearly, I stepped onto the sandy curve and inched my way down the weed-choked slope.

117

At this time of night, there was no traffic. And since there was no full moon, it was nearly pitch-black. As I approached the dark matted blur of woods just yards away, I realized I had no idea where we were. This could be Altamonte or Narcoossee, for all I knew. We could also be in one of the very few undeveloped areas just a few miles from the east coast. The road was paved but obviously not maintained. Grass, erosion, and sand had overwhelmed it. This told me we were far into the sticks.

The location, however, didn't matter. The oversized Sherman tank walking closely behind me was going to shoot me. I was going to die out here in the boonies.

I stumbled on some exposed roots and consequently felt the barrel of his pistol pressing against my lower back. "No tricks," he said flatly, and eased off the moment I straightened.

I pulled away. "It's kind of dark around here, brainiac." Since I had no other options, I no longer felt the need to be civilized—especially with a psycho thug who was about to murder me. "I don't have X-ray vision. I've never been here before, so I assume even someone with your limited perspicacity might be able to figure out that I'm not familiar with the damned terrain!"

"Cut the crap and keep movin'."

"Yes…*dear*. Whatever you say…*dear*."

The monster grunted but didn't reply.

A couple of steps later, I heard a soft click, and a small golden halo of light—possibly from a penlight—appeared just above the ground a few feet ahead, lighting my way. Ralph evidently wanted to make sure I didn't stumble again. He no doubt wanted us to be far enough away from the highway before he capped me.

I kept moving, squeezing between scrubs and avoiding tangled clusters of deadfalls. Ralph stayed close, keeping the beam of light just ahead of us.

A few minutes later, we reached a clearing, where skeletons of dead trees bent over stiffly in various stages of decomposition, their torn limbs forming the scattered piles of deadfalls covering the sandy dirt.

"Stop."

I stopped.

"Turn around."

As I turned, I saw him fastening something to the barrel of his gun.

Oh my God... A silencer...

I pulled away.

Cavanaugh, if you've got any decency left...

A rustling in the bushes just yards away made us both cringe.

***

Startled, the huge man spun to his right and kept his gun pointed straight ahead. "C'mon out!"

More rustling.

Cavanaugh? Is that you?

Ralph slowly turned. "Stay put, or I'll shoot ya right there!"

I wanted to tell him that he was going to kill me anyway, so what did it matter? I just nodded.

119

Ralph turned back to the bushes and remained in place while listening closely to the sounds carried by the gentle night breeze. I heard only silence. Then, after what seemed an eternity, he took one step forward.

More rustling.

He stopped cold. The gun in his hand twitched. "Who the fuck? Come outa there! *Now!*"

Cavanaugh's reply came in a harsh whisper. "Hey, dickhead! Come on in here and see if you can get me!"

His arm shaking slightly, Ralph popped off a quiet *phut*! into the bushes. Something dropped lightly onto the ground.

The two of us waited tensely.

A moment later, Cavanaugh's voice again: "Missed me, asshole!"

Groaning, Ralph popped off two more quick rounds. One slug slammed into something hard. The trunk of a tree, no doubt.

Silence.

Ralph took a step closer.

"Christ, you're a lousy shot!" Cavanaugh said, chuckling.

Ralph growled. Holding the pistol with both hands, he popped off three more.

"I think ya need glasses, slick. Or maybe if ya moved ten or fifteen feet closer… Lemme know if ya want me to come out and stand right in front of ya. I promise I won't move around too much…"

Roaring, Ralph darted into the bushes, shooting repeatedly.

Then it dawned on me.

This was my one and only chance.

Run, you idiot!

The panic driving me, I scurried out of there. Using instinct to dodge the deadfalls and scrub oaks, I dashed back to the limo. My body trembled as I got behind the wheel and slammed the door behind me.

Had he left the keys in the ignition? My nerves jumped erratically as I reached for them.

Hallelujah! My heart practically thrashed out of my chest.

I didn't hesitate for an instant, flicking on the ignition and slamming it into gear.

Without wasting another second, I opened it up wide, burning rubber as I tore down the bumpy country road.

***

I made it back to Oak Ridge about forty minutes later.

Ralph had apparently taken me to Narcoossee, to a wooded area not far from Lake Toho. Since I was somewhat familiar with the St. Cloud area, it wasn't difficult to find my way back to South Orange Blossom Trail from 192. Saturday night traffic slowed me down a little, but I eventually worked my way north, until I found Oak Ridge.

I parked the limo a couple of streets down from the dreaded house and four driveways down from my own car. By this time, it was past two in the morning. I was exhausted, furious, confused, and frightened. And the back of my head still hurt like the blazes. As I watched the house, I saw that the living room lights were on as well as the front porch and dining room. Apparently the two monsters were still up and about, possibly waiting to hear the latest from their trained mastodon.

Had Ralph called and told them what happened?

I wondered if I should be afraid. Then it dawned on me that unless Ralph was a certified moron, he probably wouldn't tell them what had really happened. That would surely embarrass him and perhaps even cost him his job. Cruella and the well-dressed Munchkin would both be enraged. They might even consider having Ralph removed from the gene pool. And if Ralph couldn't figure that one out on his own, he shouldn't be allowed to wander around unsupervised at all.

Then I thought about what would happen to me. What those two monsters would do. Put a contract out on my life? Report me to the cops for breaking and entering?

As I went back to the events of our last encounter, I remembered several key items that should make me feel less frightened. The most important, of course, was that they did not want the cops involved in their activities. They owned and operated a nightclub that employed the area's best-looking strippers. I had heard a few things about the place over the last few years. The words "escorts," "prostitution," "recreational drugs," "gambling," "highly-connected clients," and a few other illegal activities always seemed to go hand-in-hand with the name "Rochelle's."

No, they did not want the cops involved and would no doubt pay good money to keep something like an attempted murder out of the equation.

I knew better than worry about them. My best bet was to get away from this neighborhood as quickly as possible.

I slid out of the limo. Then, after thoroughly wiping off the door handle, steering wheel, gear shift, and keys with a handkerchief—just in case they did choose to do something that could implicate me—I got out and elbowed the door shut.

Since it was so late, no one else was up or about. I found it relatively easy to venture farther up the street without being seen. Then I snuck over to my car and got in.

I was halfway back to my Winter Park condo when I realized I wasn't the only one in the front seat.

"*Told* ya I'd getcha outa there." Cavanaugh's voice materialized beside me.

I wanted to kill the bastard. It was a damned shame he was already dead. One quick glare on my part was enough to let him know what was on my mind. It must have worked; a sudden silence followed.

However, the silence lasted only a few precious moments.

"What? No thanks, buddy, for gettin' me out of a really bad situation?"

I could not believe he said something so lame.

"A situation *you* put me into? And you're right, I have no thank you's to spare right now. But I *would* like an explanation, and I'd really appreciate it right now."

"Ya know somethin', Frank? You can be an ungrateful butthole when ya wanna be…"

"Ungrateful?" It took every ounce of self-control I could find to keep my hands on the wheel. "You must be totally insane! First, you give me this bullshit about some stripper who dumped you and has been keeping the money you wanted to give to your mother and sister. Then you direct me to a house where, according to you, this stripper lives. You don't tell me the stripper doesn't really live there. You also don't tell me a gun-toting bitch and her business partner, who looks like he came right out of Munchkin land, lives there instead. And to top it all off, these two bring in their driver, who could easily double as a psycho killer from a James Bond movie, to frisk me before knocking me out and hauling me off to a swamp, where he intended to shoot me and leave my body there for any of the local swamp creatures looking for a tasty smorgasbord. *Now* you can tell me why I should be grateful about all this."

Although another welcomed silence followed, it also did not last very long. "Well, when ya put it *that* way…"

"What other way *is* there?"

"I admit lyin' about Mona, but I didn't think those two would be home. They're always at the damn club till closin' time. It takes 'em a coupla

124

hours to do the books and fix their schedules for the next day. I had no idea they'd be comin' home so damn *early*— "

"That doesn't matter. You lied about Mona, where she lives, and the money she has that belongs to you."

"Mona did dump me, Frankie…"

"I already got that. And the name is *Frank*! And by the way, if she dumped you, she demonstrates extremely good taste, in my book."

"That was cold, Frank."

"You deserved it."

"Anyway, those two have my money, and that's the damn truth."

"I don't believe you."

"I'm serious, now."

"You can't *possibly* be serious…"

"I *am*, Frankie—Frank…"

"I still don't believe you."

"You can't believe that I got stiffed out of two thousand bucks by two crooks that own a club, rig their gamin' tables, and then have the balls to tell everyone they belong to the Chamber of Commerce?"

"Actually, I can't believe anyone who lied to me about something that nearly got me shot, dumped, and served up as gator food."

Silence.

"How can I make this up to ya, Frank?"

"Disappear. Get out of my car."

"Ya serious?"

"What do *you* think?"

125

"Well...ya sure *look* serious..."

"Fancy that..."

He didn't reply.

Since nothing else had worked so far, I decided to try and be tactful. "How about if we try this trial separation for now and see how it goes? Who knows? Maybe I'll end up feeling a little more amicable toward you if you stay away from me completely for a little while."

"Really?"

"What could it hurt?"

"How long...should I stay away, Frank?"

"Let's try a few days and see how that works."

"How will I know when to come back?"

"How about this? If you *do* come back, and I tell you to get lost again, that should be your first clue. Will *that* work?"

"You're not makin' this easy..."

"What would be the fun in that?"

"Frank—"

"You almost got me *killed*, dammit. Most people would find that hard to forget."

"I guess I deserved that one..."

"No, you deserve much worse."

"All right, I'll go. But what'll happen if ya need me?"

I wanted to laugh. "Why in heaven's name would I need you?"

"Something might happen where ya need a little help—"

"Like what?"

"Hell, I dunno. Life's weird. Look what happened to me. I'm at a bar, havin' drinks, then I walk outside a couple hours later and *boom*! I'm fuckin' dead!"

"That *was* kind of unexpected, wasn't it? Imagine that. Getting shitfaced, then stepping directly into passing traffic and actually being run over by, let's see…passing traffic…"

"Frank, work with me on this…."

"All right." I figured I should do as he said. Otherwise, this argument would take all night, and the longer we argued, the longer he stayed with me. "How about if I call for you?"

He thought that over. "That'll work. Since I won't be that far away—"

I sighed tiredly. "*That* certainly is reassuring…"

"Frank, it's gettin' harder and harder to figure out when you're tellin' the truth and when you're just kiddin'."

"Well, since you keep telling me you're my guardian angel, it's up to you to figure that one out on your own, right?"

"I guess so…"

"Bye."

"Ya want me to go now?"

"That's usually what "bye" means, right?"

"All righty, then."

Silence.

"I have this unpleasant feeling you're still here."

"You'll really let me know when it's okay to come back?"

"Damned right."

"You're not just sayin' that?"

"Nope."

"And you'll yell for me if and when ya need me?"

"Uh, yeah."

"All right. And like I said, I won't be far away."

"Bye."

"Don't be afraid to yell for me, okay?"

"Noted."

Silence.

I waited a minute or so. "Cavanaugh?"

No reply.

"You gone?"

Nothing.

I waited a little longer. "Cavanaugh?"

More silence.

"You're not the only one who can lie," I muttered at the seat next to me.

CHAPTER 5 - THE FOURTH DAY

After a few hours of restful sleep, I awoke and decided to have a breakfast of scrambled eggs, hash browns, sausage patties, and coffee at one of the local eateries on Semoran.

As I showered and dressed, I still couldn't believe Bruce Cavanaugh hadn't come back to torment me and was greatly relieved that after I'd finished my morning ritual, I remained alone in the condo.

My first instinct, of course, was that he was toying with me again. I expected to hear his voice after I'd slipped into my shirt, pulled on my pants, and went down the hall.

After some hesitation, I decided to put a test on my bravado and find out for sure. "Cavanaugh?"

No response.

"Are you here?"

Silence.

Suddenly wary, I tried another tactic. "You remember that I told you I'd call when I needed you, don't you?"

Nothing.

Still suspicious, I offered him an even more enticing morsel to consider. "If you show yourself, I promise I'll forgive you for nearly getting me killed last night…"

The resulting silence told me he had not reappeared and was not hiding anywhere in my condo.

This, of course, brightened my spirits considerably.

In just a few minutes, I was on my way to the Waffle House that awaited me just a few miles south. I wasn't wild about the eatery but was fond of their breakfast menu. They served hash browns and sausage patties just the way I liked them.

After my meal, I left the bright-eyed waitress a substantial tip, got back in my car, and was driving north on Semoran by eleven o'clock.

I had no idea how I wanted to spend my Sunday. I only knew that I wanted to spend it alone, and without any distractions or tension from Cavanaugh. If he didn't return, I'd consider it a perfect day. If he did, I would once again be forced to handle things accordingly.

My biggest complaint about all this was that, after all that had happened, I still found that I had no idea how to handle him. I wanted him gone but did not know how to go about getting it done. My anger and constant rejection took him aback but wasn't incentive enough to persuade him to disappear altogether.

I needed expert advice on this. I was tempted to use my home computer to look up a few things online, but I didn't want him to appear at the wrong moment during my research and discover what I was doing. If I had learned anything about him, it was that he would do whatever it took to convince me that he had only my best interests in mind. And any suggestion he made would hex me for the rest of my life.

I had to play this by ear. I had gotten him to stay away for a little while but knew it would only be a matter of time before he came back. I was also convinced that he would return long before I wanted him to. I didn't trust him and knew full well that he had no intention whatsoever of honoring my wishes. He would simply reappear whenever he wished—regardless of what I wanted.

This convinced me more than anything that I had to figure out some way of getting him out of my life.

For good.

***

Halfway back to the condo, I spotted a sign posted just a few yards off the main drag.

Tarot Readings by Arianna
Horoscopes
Palm Readings
"Your future lies in my hands"

The instant I saw it, I wondered why I hadn't noticed it on my way to the eatery. Other things on my mind, obviously.

The sign was stuck into the ground on the eastern side of the highway just ten feet or so from the shoulder, obscured from my view as I drove south. Traffic had been much heavier an hour or so earlier, forcing me to concentrate on the solid line in front of me. In addition, I was preoccupied with having breakfast without being pestered by

Cavanaugh and felt much too relieved and carefree to notice much of anything else.

But even though I must have passed this same sign a thousand times on my way to and from work, I never noticed it before. Now, however, I found myself gawking at it as if it were some miraculous revelation waiting patiently to inject a jolt of insight into my future. And despite any misgivings I might have had just days earlier about mediums, psychics, the afterlife, or any other astral nonsense, I experienced total fascination as I flicked on my turn signal, eased off the gas, and applied my foot to the brake pedal.

A strange glimmer of hope nudged me gently as I coasted down the narrow two-lane gravel road that led to a small, shaded parking lot facing a tiny white stucco-covered cottage nestled in a cluster of pine trees about a quarter of a mile off the main drag.

***

Two walls of the small front room were covered with built-in shelves.

Sitting on the shelves were vials, jars, cannisters, boxes, and four full rows of hardbound and paperback books on the occult and astrology. Lavender incense, burning in a soft, billowy mist from a small copper ampoule in front of the window, scented the room with a gentle sweetness.

Three straight-backed wooden chairs sat next to one another along the wall on one side of the room. Long rows of multicolored beads hung in an archway that led to another room.

I began feeling uncomfortable about being here and considered leaving. For one thing, I didn't especially believe in astrology, horoscopes, psychic phenomena, or any of that other weird stuff. However, when Bruce Cavanaugh died and came back from the dead to torment me, I found that I was beginning to believe in most anything.

Even so, I felt uneasy in this strange, unfamiliar setting. I was convinced that no one could help me, and that someone who consulted a deck of cards for spiritual guidance was not going to solve my problem. I would just have to find my answer some other way.

With a sigh, I turned and took two steps to the front door.

Just then, the clicking of the beads behind me startled me.

I spun around.

A beautiful woman appeared in the doorway. She was tall, close to six feet, with narrow shoulders and a tiny waist. Her thick black hair hung loosely, disappearing behind her shoulders. She wore a bright lime-green dress opened at the neck, revealing a white cleavage and small bosom. The white laced bottom of the dress came to within an inch or so of the floor, concealing her feet from view.

Her face was fine featured, with high cheekbones and a firm jawline. Her smooth, velvety skin made her age indeterminate. I guessed that she could be anywhere between thirty and fifty, and the fact that I saw no lines or wrinkles marking her flawless flesh made me even more uncertain. Her eyes were large, long lashed and a deep blue, and when they focused on me, I felt even more uneasy, and wondered once again why I had come here.

This was when the image of Bruce Cavanaugh popped up brightly in my head. Then, despite my initial misgivings, I suddenly believed that this strange, beautiful lady might honestly be able to help me.

"Why have you come to see me?" she asked in a soft, low-pitched voice.

I had no idea what to say. I wanted to tell her the truth, but then I remembered that this woman gave psychic readings and read palms, and another cloud of doubt rushing right back. I couldn't expect her to be able to help me with matters concerning the afterlife, could I?

"You are troubled," she said, watching me closely. "This is why you are so uncomfortable. Why you have thought twice about leaving."

I figured that was easy for anyone to figure out. My body language was obviously giving out all kinds of red flags. My discomfort and uneasiness would have registered to anyone at a cursory glance.

But how could she possibly have known I had considered leaving *twice*?

"You are troubled by a spirit."

Damn...

I quickly found that I was speechless. This was getting weirder by the second.

She continued her silent observation. I could feel her eyes on me—on my eyes, my face. She was examining me, and her expression suggested that she knew exactly what she was doing. "This spirit…it is the spirit of a man, and he will not leave you alone. Is this not true?"

I opened my mouth, but nothing would come out. This was so incredible that I had no words to describe it. This woman could actually tell what was going on by just looking at me.

"Well? I am correct?"

Once again, I tried to speak, but all I could do was nod.

"I know this is difficult."

"How…could you tell?"

"I see things."

I began growing even more uneasy.

She blinked, and I could feel the strange connection break between us. "You wish me to help you?"

"Do you think…you possibly can?"

"It is what I do." Then she turned. "Please follow me." As she pushed the beads aside, I saw that her thick black hair reached the level of her lower back.

***

This room was much smaller than the front area.

A round wooden table and two padded chairs sat in its center. A small flowery loveseat filled one corner. A white pedestal with a colorful flower arrangement in a light blue porcelain pot placed in its center highlighted the other. A large round Turkish rug covered the scuffed cedar floor. A small

135

white bookcase with two shelves crammed with hardbound books covered part of the wall on our left.

"Please sit," the woman said softly as she approached the table.

I sat in the chair. She lowered herself into the one facing me. The moment she was situated, those large deep-blue eyes began examining me again. This time they must have seen something different, which made her flinch.

"What's wrong?" I asked.

"I have just sensed something dark and cold surrounding your aura."

I looked around the room but saw only the two of us.

"What is it you wish me to do?" she asked.

"It's kind of hard…to explain."

"It might make things simpler for both of us if you told me what has brought you here."

"It's a long story."

"If you would like me to help you, I must know what we are dealing with."

She was right; I would have to tell her everything. But when it came right down to it, I found that explaining this madness had become exceedingly difficult. Even so, I took a breath and forced myself to struggle through it.

I told her everything—from when Bruce Cavanaugh, as a child, started making my childhood difficult, followed by his death and resurrection twenty years later, and ending with my harrowing escape in St. Cloud from Ralph the Human Tank.

Arianna listened intently, her passionate eyes focused on me, her tense expression revealing nothing. I couldn't tell if she believed me or thought I was hallucinating. Some inner sense told me she wouldn't dismiss my story entirely. Perhaps it had something to do with her initial reaction to my presence in the main room, or the fact that she did this sort of thing for a living and had no doubt heard some wild, crazy things. But what mattered to me was that she remained sitting there, expressionless, long after I'd finished.

"Unbelievable, huh?" I hoped I was right about her original evaluation of me.

Without a word, she lowered her hands beneath the surface of the table and produced something that must have been lying in a drawer or shelf. It was a small white box. She removed the top and pulled out its contents. In her hand lay a thick deck of what looked like playing cards. Tarot cards? I could only guess. But judging by her serenity, plus the expert way she handled the cards, I figured she knew what she was doing.

"Tarot cards?" I asked.

She placed them face-down on the table. Then, with a smooth sweep of her hand, she pushed them open, until the deck was spread out in a perfect semicircle. Since she had executed this in a swift, well-coordinated motion, I guessed she'd done this thousands of times before. "These are angel tarot cards. This exercise will determine if the spirit troubling you is truly a guardian angel."

"You don't think he is, do you?"

"I strongly suspect he is not."

"How can you know?"

"Guardians never act in this fashion. They do not show themselves or let themselves be heard in any conventional way. If they did, they would not be vulgar or arrogant. And no, they certainly do not put their hosts into extreme jeopardy."

She was talking about the incident with Shelley and Russ sending me away to be killed and dumped in the woods. But even so, I decided to be the good guy and give Cavanaugh some leeway.

"Well, he *is* only recently dead. He even admitted that he's new at this."

"This does not matter. His actions have told me all I need to know. I am strongly convinced he has not been accepted by the proper side."

"Side?" I had no idea what she meant.

She nodded grimly.

"Which side is that?"

"The realm of light and love—of happiness and the state of bliss, delight, and peace. Many refer to this experience as Nirvana, or the White Light."

Her statement made me wonder if she meant Cavanaugh had fallen into Hell. "You mean—"

She lowered her eyes to the cards and stiffened.

"What…did you see?"

"Darkness..." She whispered the word.

"In the cards?"

"*On* them. Covering them. Hovering just above them. This darkness is trying to smother them."

"Are you sure?"

"Pick a card. Flip it over."

138

Hesitantly I reached for one. It immediately slid away from my fingers. My first instinct was that static energy had caused it to pull away. "It doesn't...I can't...pick the damned thing up!"

"It is the darkness." She continued staring intently at the cards. "It has created a barrier. This barrier is preventing you from touching them."

"The darkness you see on them?"

"The darkness on your hand."

I pulled my hand back and gawked at it.

"You cannot see it."

"But *you* can?"

She nodded.

I was afraid to ask. "Do you see...anything...*else*?"

She didn't respond right off. Then, "I am afraid so."

I could feel my resolve vanishing quickly. "Please...tell me what's going on."

"It is your aura. It has dimmed considerably since you first came to see me."

"My aura?"

"It is the field of illumination surrounding you, connecting you to the other spheres. It reveals your moods, the state of your spirit, your feelings."

"You can actually see mine?"

"It is one of my strengths. It is generally accepted that the lighter, softer colors of the rainbow signify a direct connection with the White Forces of the universe. By the same token, darker colors signify a strong link to the forces of the Darkworld."

139

"What color…is mine?" I could barely get the words out.

"It was pale when I first saw you."

"W-Was?" I could feel the blood turning cold in my veins.

"It has dimmed considerably in the last fifteen minutes."

"Wh-What exactly…does that mean?"

"The spirit tormenting you—that same spirit claiming to be your guardian angel—is coming for you as we speak."

***

I felt myself shrinking into the seat.

Cavanaugh, damn him, was coming back. I should have known he wouldn't abide by our agreement. And why should he? Regardless of what he had told me, he was *not* my guardian angel. I wasn't stupid. Even though I wasn't even sure I believed in such a concept, I could tell something was bad about him.

It made no sense. Would a guardian angel torment me? Embarrass me? Lie to me? Place me in a situation that would put my life in extreme danger?

None of that mattered right now. The only thing I cared about was that the bastard was coming back. Though he said he wouldn't return until I called for him, he'd proven several times that he obviously had no intention of keeping his word. To me, this clearly showed that he truly did not care about my well-being.

I knew right then that I had to get things cleared up before he returned. I had no idea how long I had. I knew only that once he came back, more trouble would plague me.

"He's...not back yet...*is* he?"

Arianna didn't reply right off. She seemed to be listening. She sat quite still, her head tilted, her eyes closed. She seemed to be meditating, or whatever psychics did to pick up the vibes in the air. I had no idea if she could help me get rid of Cavanaugh. I just hoped she could help me through this while I still retained a semblance of sanity.

She finally opened her eyes. "It shan't be long."

"Before he gets here, can you tell me anything that might help me?"

"I can only tell you what I feel and what my aura has picked up. What I have gotten so far is that this spirit has been claimed by the dark forces. The fallen."

"How can you tell?"

"I am experiencing a heavy darkness drifting into our sphere. It is accompanied by sourness, with an unpleasant quality that is making me slightly nauseous."

"I don't feel it."

"I do, but I am a sensitive. I also strongly suspect Tiamanicus—or one of his many messengers—is somehow involved."

"Tia...manicus?"

"He is the demon prince of deception. He claims new souls and sends his legion of inferior demons to claim mortals. He is one of the fallen

141

Seraphim. While in Heaven, he was working for the white angel Blandine when he decided that he wanted to fashion a connection between the corporeal world and the ethereal realm. He attempted a fusion of the dream world and reality—which, of course, would most certainly cause mayhem and mass confusion among spirits and mortals everywhere."

"What happened?"

"The white forces would not tolerate his diabolical plan. They sent an army of angels to intervene, and Tiamanicus was sent directly to Hell."

"Then this dude is sending his guys up here to confuse us?"

"He has apparently been fashioning his connection in the Darkworld and has no doubt been successful. In this case, I fear that he has targeted your friend—"

"He isn't my friend."

"Whoever this troubled soul is, he could now quite possibly be a pawn of Tiamanicus."

"Does Cavanaugh know what's going on?"

"I have no idea. As I have said, these demons are masters of deception. As is their practice, they approached him the moment he left his physical body. In sensing his weaknesses, they decided he would be a useful candidate for their evil. They no doubt deceived him into thinking he could be a messenger on the white side if he hosted a mortal. Since you were obviously a strong influence from his early past, he picked you. And since your visit to his grave alerted him, convincing him that you sympathized with him, he decided to repay you this way. If he has no idea as to the identity of the messengers that approached him, he might not even realize what he is doing."

"And if he does?"

"Then this will be even more difficult to deal with."

"Are you saying you'll help me?"

"I shall try. I have no idea how I can accomplish this, but I cannot in good conscience permit a client to be tormented by a spirit of the dark side without doing what I can to prevent it."

"You're telling me I'm a client?"

"Once you pay me, you are."

"How much do you want?"

"How much is this worth to you?"

"*Way* the hell more than I've got."

"Give me whatever amount you decide, and I shall start working for you."

"All right, but—"

"You had better give it to me quickly," she said, her eyes growing.

"W-What's…going on?"

She closed her eyes. "The darkness…he shall be here in just moments."

I jammed my hand into my pocket, pulled out my cash, and handed it to her.

She took the bills without looking at them, stuffed them down her cleavage, closed her eyes, and lowered her head.

Just then, I heard Cavanaugh's voice uncomfortably close behind me.

***

"A *tarot reader*, Frankie? Ya shittin' me?"

Cavanaugh's irritating voice resonated in the room about five feet on my right, in front of the flower arrangement. "Why the hell would ya— *whoa*! What a fox! Wow... Tell me you ain't bangin' away at *that* number and I'll tell ya you're *really* full of shit!"

"You're back," I said flatly, sighing. "I thought we had an understanding."

"I've been thinkin' about that ever since ya tossed me outa your condo. Guess what I decided."

"Let me try a long shot. You decided to come back anyway?"

"Your momma didn't raise any morons, did she, Frankie?"

"I hope not. And the name—for the hundredth time—is *Frank!*"

"Tell me about this babe, Frankie, my boy..." The fact that his voice had shifted a few feet closer to the table suggested that he had drifted over to where Arianna was sitting. "Does she...I mean, are you and her...ya doin' the horizontal tango with this bimbo?"

His obscene chuckle made my blood boil.

Arianna's expression did not change. She remained sitting there, gazing at the cards spread out on the table. She seemed to be in some sort of trance. This told me she couldn't hear Cavanaugh and what he was saying about her. This made me feel a little better.

"You know you're an asshole, don't you?" I told him.

"People have been tellin' me that all my life, but ya know what? I'm dead now, so callin' me names just don't matter anymore. See, I can do whatever I want, and—"

"He is definitely *not* your guardian angel." Arianna was now staring directly at me. Her expression was grim.

"What's she talkin' about, Frankie-boy? This bimbo's seriously hot, but she's just about as dumb as a sack of wet beans."

"She knows what she's talking about. This is what she does."

"Frankie-boy, two things ya need to pound into that melon and keep there. One, I'm your guardian angel, and two, this babe's lyin' to ya."

"Actually, *you're* the one who's been lying to me."

"Prove it."

"He wants us to prove it," I told her.

Arianna continued staring at me. "This will be very simple."

"Really?"

"Yes. Pick a card."

"Wait a damn minute." Cavanaugh sounded irritated. "What's she talkin' about? What the hell *is* all this? She wants to prove somethin' about me with *Tarot cards*? Seriously? Ya know what they say about *them*, don'tcha?"

"What do they say?"

"She's a con artist, Frankie. How much did ya pay 'er?"

"He wants to know how much I paid you," I told her.

"He is trying to convince you to distrust me. Do not listen to him."

"I can do that. In fact, that's what I've been longing to do ever since he came back from the dead."

"Listen, Frankie..." Cavanaugh's tone had changed. For some reason, he sounded nervous, agitated. "I'm on your side. This babe...like I said, she's hot, and she's got a delicious bod, but—"

"Pick a card," she said again.

I picked one. This time, it didn't slide away from my touch.

She flipped it over.

The angel's name was Haniel and was depicted by a beautiful blonde with wings.

Arianna held the card up to her face. "This Guide is the Angel of Harmonious Love. Under her guidance, you will be blessed with positive vibes and a wonderfully warm aura. Love has an essential place in your life. Haniel will teach you that there are two forms of love that you have been giving to others: one to your family, your friends and your lover, and another to the world around you. If you are going through a tough time, Haniel will help restore your faith in the universal sense of love. Trust yourself and your feelings. By expressing your love, you will find the path to happiness and harmony."

"Harmonious fuckin' *love*?" Cavanaugh sounded like he was about to be sick. "What the fuck is this bitch talkin' about?"

"She's discrediting you. I believe every word she says. And she's not a bitch."

"You're an idiot, Frankie. You picked the wrong card."

I stared at Arianna. "He just said I picked the wrong card."

She returned it to the deck. "Pick another, then."

I picked another card, this time from the other end of the deck, and pulled it toward me.

Arianna reached for it, flipped it over, and picked it up. "This says that your Guide is Cambriel, the Angel of Ideals. You apparently lack focus and are inclined to daydream, and do not fully realize what is happening around you. If you did have a true guardian angel, Cambriel would be the one to help you restore balance in your life and the world around you."

"Wait a fuckin' minute!" Cavanaugh's voice grew raspy with anger. "This really sucks. You can't take these stupid cards seriously. They got nothin' to do with me or what's goin' on with you and me. She's a scam artist, I tell ya. A phoney."

His voice had grown slightly softer in volume.

Unaffected by Cavanaugh's outburst, Arianna continued reading. "Cambriel will help you develop empathy. With her assistance, you will make the most of your qualities. You are a person full of ideals. You want to do great things because you have a deep perception of the world around you. You have great potential. If you come to doubt it, Cambriel will restore the strength to believe in yourself." She dropped the card and gently nudged it back into the deck. "Does this sound anything like the spirit standing behind me right now, looking down the front of my dress?"

"Whoa!" Cavanaugh's voice suggested surprise. "How the fuck did she...she *is* good, ain't she, Frankie-boy? She may be a scammer, but she's good."

"I know she's good. And she's *not* a scammer. Why do you think I'm sitting here with her?"

"Listen, Frankie...we really need to talk this over. Sure, she found a bunch of shit in those cards, but that don't mean anything, does it? They're just *cards*, for Chrissakes!"

"It means a lot to *me*..."

"What the hell's it mean?"

"For one thing, it means you've been lying to me."

"We're talking *cards*, here!"

"They mean a lot."

"They're just *cards*. They prob'ly make 'em in *China*, dammit... Wanna believe *cards* over what's happened between you and me?"

"I believe whatever this lady tells me."

"Frankie, I know what you're doin'. I know ya wanna get in this bimbo's pants and all, and I don't blame ya one bit. See, if I was still walkin' around like before, I'd seriously wanna slip inside those drawers, too. Matter of fact, once I got into 'em, I'd stay there as long as I could. But this is bullshit. She's lyin' to ya, my man. Ya really need to *listen* to me!"

"I'd like to, but she's showing me a lot of things here. And the stuff she's showing me makes a lot of sense."

"Frankie, she's just a fuckin' *Tarot reader!*"

"You've been lying to me, Bruce."

"Listen here—"

"You're not my guardian angel at all, are you?"

"Frankie—"

"Admit it. You've been doing a number on me, haven't you?"

"Whaddya mean? Look how I saved your butt—and more than once, dammit!"

To Arianna, I said, "Guardian angels don't curse, do they?"

She sighed. "I should think that would be obvious."

I sat back in my seat and waited for a reply.

"Forget that shit, Frankie. I'm upset, goddammit..."

"Tell me about the first time you saved my butt."

A chuckle. "You remember that, don'tcha?"

"Refresh my memory."

"It happened right outside your condo. You just picked up your mail. That bike woulda turned your ass into an overcooked barbecued hamburger if I hadn't—"

149

"Hadn't what? Made me drop two envelopes so I could move out of the way of the motorcycle you deliberately sabotaged?"

"Dammit, Frankie, it didn't *happen* that way. It didn't happen that way *at all*!"

His voice sounded farther away.

"Tell me you didn't sabotage that motorcycle. Tell me you didn't do something to the driver."

"I don't know what you're talkin' about!"

"You sabotaged that bike and lied to me about it. You did it so I would think you saved my life. But you didn't save my life at all. You merely sacrificed the life of that innocent kid just so I'd start trusting you. That was low, Bruce. That was just about as low as it gets. I can't see a legitimate spirit doing something like that. I can't see anyone with a heart and soul—or a conscience—do something like that. Am I right, Arianna?"

"Angels in the white light do only good," she said. "They are incapable of hurting the innocent."

"Don't listen to her, Frankie. She doesn't know what the hell she's talkin' about!"

"Let's get off that and onto that other issue."

"What other issue?"

"This would be that second time you saved my butt—as you obviously like describing it. Look what you did when you sent me to that home on Oak Ridge…"

"I *told* ya what happened there. And don't forget—I got ya outa there before that big ape had the chance to shoot your ass!"

150

"He would not have been able to shoot my ass—or knock me out and then stuff me in the trunk of that limousine—if you hadn't stuck me in that situation in the first place."

"But—"

"But what?"

"I saved your butt, Frankie..." His voice sounded farther away.

"You're *not* my guardian angel."

"Frankie—"

"You're no one's guardian angel."

"You have no idea what you're—"

"You're from the dark side. Arianna told me all about it, and I believe her."

"Why would ya believe a scammer over me when I've already saved your—"

"There's nothing positive...or pleasant...or hopeful...or even remotely joyful...surrounding your aura. You've definitely gone over to the dark side. They own you. You either know it and are lying to me or don't know it and are too stupid to be able to figure it all out on your own."

"You can't possibly believe—"

"I *do* believe it."

"She brainwashed ya, you idiot. You have no idea what she's—"

"Pick one last card." Arianna was staring at me again.

"What the hell's one last card gonna do?" Cavanaugh asked, his voice even softer, less distinct.

"I have no idea, but I intend to find out."

151

"This sucks, Frankie. This really and truly sucks, big-time."

Focusing on the deck, I lowered my hand.

"Don't do it, Frankie…"

This time, one of the cards began sliding again, but in the direction of my hand. I stopped cold.

"Don't…" Cavanaugh sounded even farther away.

Arianna nodded. The hint of a smile touched her full lips.

I lowered my hand another inch. The card slid one or two more inches, until it was directly beneath my palm. I picked it up and looked at it.

"What does it say?" she asked.

"It says, "Your Guide is the Angel of Strength. You currently are standing at an impasse. Your heart is closed because of something you did or something someone did to you. Your angel Zeruch will help you reclaim your life. Positive energy will be placed into your soul to help you confront your demons. If you have caused someone harm, you want to repair the harm you have created. If you are the one who has suffered harm, Zeruch will help the spirit who hurt you ask for forgiveness. This way, you both will be back on a good foundation.""

Arianna smiled brightly.

"This is my true guardian angel?"

"Zeruch is your guardian. You are in excellent hands."

I sighed in relief and relaxed in my seat. I wanted to tell Bruce that I forgave him and that even though I knew he was no angel, I understood why he'd done what he'd done.

"Bruce?"

Silence.

"Bruce? I forgive you."

Nothing.

I met Arianna's eyes. Her half-smile told me that she no longer felt Bruce's presence. And neither did I.

The last thing I heard was his voice. It sounded very, very far away, and so muffled, I could barely understand him.

"Get...hell away...me. Dammit. Leave me. Please. Can't..."

A moment later, the sudden silence grew heavy in the room.

***

"He's...*gone*?"

I couldn't believe it. I even found that I had trouble saying the word aloud. *Gone. Disappeared. Not here anymore.* I just couldn't quite accept the notion that Arianna and I were alone in the room.

"Yes. Of course he is." Arianna gathered the cards together neatly, put the deck back in the box, and returned it to its former place beneath the tabletop. "He has been defeated."

"That's all it took? Picking a few cards from a deck?"

"It was a little more than that." Genuine pride showed in Arianna's beautiful blue eyes. "And it wasn't just a deck of cards."

153

It took me a few moments to realize what she'd just said. "It was that White Light thing, wasn't it?"

"The White Light is very powerful."

"I guess the angels got together and just sent him away."

Arianna nodded. "Zeruch had quite a lot to do with it."

"You mean—"

"He made sure you were given positive strength."

"I didn't even feel anyone else's presence…"

"He was there, believe me."

"Right here? In this room?"

"Standing there right beside you. He was the one dimming the darkness surrounding the fallen spirit."

I still couldn't believe how quickly it had happened. "Then Zeruch and the other angels sent Cavanaugh…back down?"

"His troubled spirit is now where it belongs."

"And I didn't have to do anything."

Arianna smiled and shook her head. "You did more than you thought."

I had no idea what she was talking about. "What exactly was *that*?"

"You believed."

It sounded much too simple. "And that was *all* that was necessary?"

She put her hands together and rested them on the table. "Demons of deception are powerless when their victims discover the truth. This is when the light coming from their true guardian grows within them and pushes the darkness away. The arsenal of the dark angels is strengthened with lies and half-truths, but when faced with truth, honesty, logic, and reason, their defenses collapse, revealing their true motives. You sensed his reaction to me when he first appeared. He immediately recognized trouble and intimidation and tried covering it with vulgarity, nasty remarks, and off-color humor. I could sense the fear gushing from his aura."

"You felt his presence when he was standing behind you?"

"Of course."

"You didn't let on."

"It was my best and most effective defense against the dark forces. When dealing with the Darkworld, we must do whatever we can to let them assume they have the advantage. This defense, combined with what we discovered in the cards and what you have learned, was enough to defeat him. And when you summoned Zeruch, Talimanicus' spirit no longer possessed power over your aura."

"Then Cavanaugh no longer exists?"

"Not to you."

"Good. This is all I care about."

"Now he must find another spirit—or mortal—who will become a pawn to his deception."

"What if he doesn't?"

"He must. Otherwise, Talimanicus will send him to a different demon, and if he does not prove himself with this successor, he shall be sent down into the darkness to remain there forever, alone and isolated."

"That sounds harsh."

"It is, but since he has obviously picked the dark side, he must abide by whatever they dictate."

"Then I'm finally free of him?"

"Definitely."

"How can I possibly repay you?"

"You have already paid me."

"It wasn't nearly enough."

"You might wish to add something to the bowl in the front room. It sits on the table next to the door. It is marked "*Donations*.""

"I think I can handle that."

"Actually, my true payment was that I was able to rid a nice man of a meddlesome demon. For me, that is more than enough."

"You really are a terrific lady."

She didn't reply, but I could see her cheeks reddening.

"Thank you again," I said.

She took my hand. Her touch was warm and strong, and made me feel good inside.

EPILOGUE

I got back in my car, went down the gravel drive, then pulled back onto Semoran Boulevard.

On the way back to my apartment, I kept glancing at the passenger seat, fearful that Cavanaugh's troubled spirit had somehow returned, and that he would resume tormenting me. I expected to hear his voice, his disgusting chuckling. For an instant, I thought I did. But as I stopped at the first light, I listened carefully but heard nothing. I glanced at the empty seat once again and sincerely hoped his spirit was not actually there.

Still, I realized I would never rest again until I made sure.

"Cavanaugh?"

Silence.

"You deserved what you got, you know."

More silence.

"Sorry, but you gave me no choice."

Again, silence.

I decided to make one last desperate attempt with something that was sure to entice him if his spirit had indeed returned.

"Bruce, I'll forgive you for everything you've done, and I'll even consider you my guardian angel, if you just tell me you're sitting here with me."

The soft, steady hum of the engine was the only thing I heard.

Greatly relieved, I let out a giant sigh. I told myself it was over. Cavanaugh was where he should be, and I would never see or hear him again. And if I was lucky, I wouldn't even stumble upon his presence in the Afterlife.

As these thoughts brought about a fresh rush of sunshine to my head, I focused on the drive home and told myself that, for the first time since my foolish trip to the cemetery, I would spend the rest of my evening—and my life—in peace.

By myself.

Without a nasty spirit from the Dark World following me around.

OTHER WORKS BY DAVID BERARDELLI

THE APPRENTICE
DEMON CHASER
DEMON CHASER II
STEPPING OUT OF MY GRAVE
COLORS
WORKING FOR A MOB BOSS
DEMON CHASER III
IN ANOTHER REALM
BEYOND RECOGNITION
THE NIGHTMARE COLLECTOR
HIDDEN
BEYOND GUILT
A RIPPLE IN TIME
DEMON CHASER IV
ENCHANTMENT
DEMON CHASER V
REDEMPTION
AWAKENED
THE PLANNING COMMITTEE
WINTER SCENE

Titles available through:
Fiction4All
www.fiction4all.com